"I'm shutting you down," Parker said, his eyes cold, his voice hard.

"You don't have the authority to do that," Melody exclaimed.

"I'll get it." Tension tightened Parker's muscles as he stared at the drugs sitting on the shelf in the locker. It figured the youth center would be too good to be true. Guess the rumor mill was correct.

Was Melody dealing drugs out of the center? Disappointment flooded his system, yet he had a hard time reconciling those thoughts with the woman standing next to him. The shock in her eyes, the distress on her face couldn't be an act. Could it?

If she were guilty of dealing drugs through the center, she'd have thought up some excuse to refuse opening the locker. But there'd been no excuses, no hesitation.

He'd give her the benefit of the doubt.

TEXAS K-9 UNIT:

These lawmen solve the toughest cases with the help of their brave canine partners

Tracking Justice—Shirlee McCoy, January 2013
Detection Mission—Margaret Daley, February 2013
Guard Duty—Sharon Dunn, March 2013
Explosive Secrets—Valerie Hansen, April 2013
Scent of Danger—Terri Reed, May 2013
Lone Star Protector—Lenora Worth, June 2013

Books by Terri Reed

Love Inspired Suspense

*Double Deception
 Beloved Enemy
 Her Christmas Protector
*Double Jeopardy
*Double Cross
*Double Threat Christmas
 Her Last Chance
 Chasing Shadows
 Covert Pursuit
 Holiday Havoc
   "Yuletide Sanctuary"
 Daughter of Texas
†The Innocent Witness
†The Secret Heiress
 The Deputy's Duty

†The Doctor's Defender
†The Cowboy Target
 Scent of Danger

*The McClains
†Protection Specialists

Love Inspired

Love Comes Home
A Sheltering Love
A Sheltering Heart
A Time of Hope
Giving Thanks for Baby
Treasure Creek Dad

TERRI REED

At an early age Terri Reed discovered the wonderful world of fiction and declared she would one day write a book. Now she is fulfilling that dream and enjoys writing for Love Inspired Books. Her second book, *A Sheltering Love,* was a 2006 RITA® Award finalist and a 2005 National Readers' Choice Award finalist. Her book *Strictly Confidential,* book five in the Faith at the Crossroads continuity series, took third place in the 2007 American Christian Fiction Writers Book of the Year Award, and *Her Christmas Protector* took third place in 2008. She is an active member of both Romance Writers of America and American Christian Fiction Writers. She resides in the Pacific Northwest with her college-sweetheart husband, two wonderful children and an array of critters. When not writing, she enjoys spending time with her family and friends, gardening and playing with her dogs.

You can write to Terri at P.O. Box 19555 Portland, OR 97280. Visit her on the web at www.loveinspiredauthors.com or email her at terrireed@sterling.net.

SCENT OF DANGER

TERRI REED

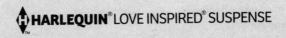

HARLEQUIN® LOVE INSPIRED® SUSPENSE

Special thanks and acknowledgment to Terri Reed
for her contribution to the Texas K-9 Unit miniseries.

Recycling programs
for this product may
not exist in your area.

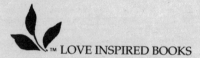

™ LOVE INSPIRED BOOKS

ISBN-13: 978-0-373-67557-9

SCENT OF DANGER

www.LoveInspiredBooks.com

Printed in U.S.A.

The Lord is my light and my salvation:
Whom shall I fear? The Lord is the strength
of my life: Of Whom shall I be afraid?
—*Psalms* 27:1

Thank you to my fellow Texas K-9 authors:
Shirlee McCoy, Margaret Daley, Sharon Dunn,
Valerie Hansen and Lenora Worth.
You made working on this series fun.

ONE

Detective Melody Zachary halted abruptly at the sight of her office door cracked open. Unease slithered down her spine. She'd locked the door last night when she left the Sagebrush Youth Center. She always did.

Pushing back her suit jacket, she unlatched her weapon from the holster at her hip and withdrew the Sig Sauer. She pushed the door wide with the toe of her heeled boot. Stepping inside the darkened room, she reached with her free hand for the overhead light switch and froze.

A shadow moved.

Not a shadow. A man.

Dressed from head to toe in black. Black gloves, black ski mask...

Black eyes.

Not just the irises, but the white part of his eyes, as well.

Her heart stalled.

Palming her piece in both hands, she aimed her weapon. "Halt! Police!"

The intruder dove straight at her. She didn't have time to react, to pull the trigger, before he slammed into her chest, knocking her backward against the wall. Her head smacked hard, sending pain slicing through her brain. The air rushed out of her lungs.

The man bolted through the open doorway and disappeared, leaving only the echo of his black, rubber-soled tennis shoes squishing against the linoleum and bouncing off the walls of the hallway.

Ignoring the pain pounding in her head, Melody pushed away from the wall. For a moment, her off-balance equilibrium sent the world spinning.

The exit door at the end of the hall banged shut. She grimaced. He was escaping.

Forcing herself to move, Melody chased after the intruder. As founder and co-director of the youth center, she'd come in this morning expecting to get a little work done before heading to the police station to start her shift. She hadn't been prepared for a smackdown and footrace.

The blood surging through her brought the world into a sharp focus she didn't experience anywhere else in her life except on the job. It had been a while since she'd had to chase a perp. And never from the youth center.

This place was supposed to be safe, for the kids who sought help and for the volunteers who ran the center.

Out on the sidewalk, she searched for the trespasser. Sagebrush Boulevard was empty. There was no sign of a person dressed in black. At seven in the morning on a Tuesday, Sagebrush, Texas, was barely coming to life.

At the end of town, the spire of the white community church gleamed in the early morning May sunlight, like a beacon of hope. A stark contrast to the dark figure who'd assaulted her. She sent up a silent prayer of protection, for herself, for the youth center and for the citizens of Sagebrush.

A cynical voice in her head taunted, *Would God listen?*

As much as she hated to admit it, she didn't know. He certainly hadn't listened to her pleas when her marriage fell apart and her ex-husband abandoned her to go "find himself."

Holstering her weapon and pulling her tailored jacket closed, she retraced her steps and entered Sagebrush Youth Center's single-story brick building.

She stopped in her office doorway surveying the scene. Irritation raced through her. The place had been ransacked. The filing cabinet had been emptied, the files strewn all over. The pictures of her family had been knocked off the desk.

Her heart squeezed tight at the sight of her sister's face smiling up at her from one of the images. Her arm was slung over her then twelve-year-old son's shoulders. A time when they'd been happy. Alive.

Forcing back the sadness, she continued her perusal. Books ranging from popular fiction to nonfiction teenage psychology had been pulled down from the shelves and lay haphazardly on the floor. The open desk drawers appeared to have been rifled through.

A cardboard box lay toppled upside down, the contents spilling out. Her nephew's name was written across the side in big bold letters. She didn't need a paper inventory of the box. She had the contents memorized. The files full of witness testimonies, and Daniel's effects at the time of his death had been in that box. All that was left of a life cut too short.

A sense of violation cramped her chest. She was used to investigating this sort of vandalism, not being the victim herself.

She was no one's victim. Her fist clenched.

She would find the person who broke in, and discover what they'd wanted. She tapped her foot, impatient to get in there and see what had been taken.

But protocol had to be followed.

Yanking her cell phone out of the backpack-style purse she always carried, she dialed the Sagebrush police dispatch non-emergency number.

"Sagebrush Police Department." Cathy Rodriquez, the day dispatch operator answered in her no-nonsense tone.

"Cathy, it's Detective Zachary. I need a crime-scene unit at the youth center. My office has been broken into."

"Were you hurt, Melody?"

"I'm fine." She wouldn't mention the throbbing headache. The last thing she needed was to be coddled. She'd find some pain reliever in the nurse's station once things settled down. "I surprised the intruder, but he got away."

"I'll let the higher ups know what's going on."

"Thanks, I appreciate it." Melody hung up and leaned against the doorjamb. Despite the doubts that at times tried to rob her of faith, she sent up a silent prayer of thanksgiving that the intruder hadn't been armed. This scene could have gone down very differently.

The sound of footsteps sent a fresh wave of adrenaline pumping through her veins. She whipped around, her hand going to her weapon.

"Melody?"

At the sight of her volunteer co-director and fellow Sagebrush police officer coming toward her, she let out a tense breath. Jim Wheaton always wore the navy blue Sagebrush Police Department uniform, claiming the visual reminder of authority helped keep the kids in line.

Nearing fifty and single, Jim spent more time at the center, whether he was on duty or off, than any other volunteer. He claimed it was because he didn't trust the teens not to cause trouble, but Melody suspected he liked the company even if he wouldn't admit it.

"You're here early again today," he said, coming to a halt a few paces away.

She usually stopped by Arianna's Diner for a pastry and cup of coffee before heading to the station, but ever since her nephew's grave had been desecrated last month, she hadn't had much of an appetite. Keeping herself occupied gave her less time to think.

Besides, the diner was closed now that the owner, Arianna Munson, had been killed after being linked to the crime lord, known only by the police as The Boss.

For the past several years, a crime wave had terrorized the citizens of Sagebrush. The mastermind behind the crime syndicate was a faceless, nameless entity that even the thugs who worked for The Boss feared.

This man was at the top of the police department's most-wanted list. Especially after the crime syndicate kidnapped Rio, the three-year-old German shepherd partner of the K-9 unit's captain. The whole department was on high alert looking for the canine.

She could have used a dog like Rio today. Maybe she should look into getting a K-9 partner for the center. A nice big dog with sharp teeth. "Hey, Jim. I interrupted someone breaking into my office. They made a mess of things."

His gray eyes clouded with concern. "You okay?"

"Just a bruised ego." And a knock to the noggin. Nothing she couldn't handle.

"Let me see." He tried to push past her.

Her arm shot out and blocked him from entering. "I'm waiting for the CSU team."

He scowled. "It was probably a kid looking for some loose change."

Melody shook her head. "Guy was too big, too strong to be a teen."

"You get a look at his face?"

"I didn't."

The center's front door opened. A small dog with his black nose pressed to the ground entered. Melody recognized the beagle as Sherlock, part of the K-9 unit. He wore a vest with the Sagebrush Police Department emblem over his light brown and white coat. A harness attached to a leash led to the handsome man at the other end. Melody blinked.

What were Narcotics Detective Parker Adams and his K-9 partner doing here?

The dog was adorable with his floppy ears and big round eyes.

Much like his handler.

She didn't know the narcotics detective well. She worked for the homicide division, mostly cold cases, while he was part of the Sagebrush's elite K-9 unit. Their paths hadn't crossed much, though she'd noticed him at the police station.

Hard not to take notice when he filled out his uniform nicely with broad shoulders and trim waist. She liked the way he wore his dark hair swept back from his forehead and his warm brown eyes appeared kind whenever he glanced her way.

He wasn't much taller than she, but he had a commanding presence that she found disconcerting. Though why, she wasn't sure. Growing up the daughter of a cop, there were few people who intimidated her. But something about the handsome officer made her pay attention.

Two crime-scene-unit techs filed in behind Parker carrying in their equipment. Considering the police station was at the other end of the block, Melody wasn't surprised how quickly they'd arrived. She just didn't understand why Parker had responded to her call.

The CSU team approached, each member wearing a dark blue Sagebrush Police Department windbreaker. Parker hung back, letting his dog sniff the floor, the thresholds of the closed classroom doors, the lockers.

"Hey, Melody," said Rose Bigsby, a stocky woman with short blond curls and wire-rimmed glasses perched on her short nose. "Report came in that you had a break-in."

Melody gestured to the open door of her office. "In there."

Clay Gregson nodded to Jim and then smiled shyly at Melody as he moved past her to enter her office. The tall and lean CSU technician wasn't much on small talk, something the officers of SPD were used to. Rose, on the other hand, made up for her partner's lack of conversation just fine. Rose followed him in and started the process of looking for anything that would lead them to ID the intruder.

"Any idea who broke in?" Parker asked as he and his dog approached. "What was he looking for?"

Melody frowned. "I have no idea who the guy was or what he was after."

"What are you doing here, Adams?" Jim asked.

"Captain McNeal thought it'd be a good idea for Sherlock here to check out the center," Parker replied evenly. "Considering."

Her defenses stirred. "Considering what?"

He met her gaze. His dark eyes intense, probing. "The rumors of drugs being dealt out of here."

Her hackles rose like the feathers of a peacock on high alert. She'd been battling that particular thread of gossip since the center opened. She routinely searched the building and kept a close eye on the kids. She was certain there were no drugs on the premises. "We have a strict no-drugs policy. Any offenders will be prosecuted to the full extent of the law."

Parker shrugged. "Then there's nothing to worry about. Sherlock shouldn't find anything. He's got the best nose in the state, and it's never wrong."

"I've got to go to the station," Jim said abruptly and headed for the exit.

Watching him hustle out the door, Melody frowned. He'd just arrived. She shrugged off her coworker's strange behavior. Even though she was fond of Jim, she'd long ago decided she would never figure out the male species.

Or teenagers. Starting the youth center had been her attempt to help the kids of Sagebrush so they wouldn't end up like her nephew. At sixteen, Daniel had gotten mixed up with drugs, dealing and using, by all accounts. He'd ended up dead because of it. During a standoff with the police, he'd been wounded in the leg by Captain Slade McNeal and then shot in the heart by an unknown sniper. The assassin was never caught.

Saving other teens from Daniel's fate had become her mission in life.

However, that didn't mean she understood the teens or their thought processes. Thankfully, there were tons of books on the subject. If she could prevent even one teen from ending up addicted to drugs like Daniel, she'd feel she succeeded.

Her gaze strayed back to the mess in her office. Rose knelt beside the lamp and dusted black powder over the surface. The flash of a camera momentarily brightened the room as Clay photographed the crime scene.

What had the intruder been looking for?

"Did you get a look at the perp?" Parker asked, drawing her attention.

"No, he wore a ski mask."

"With blacked-out eyes?"

Surprise washed through her. "Yes. Very freaky. How did you know?"

"We've had a run-in with a guy wearing a ski

mask and some kind of eyewear that blacks out the whites of his eyes. Did he take anything?"

Absorbing that information, she turned her gaze once again to the box labeled with her nephew's name. Would she find something missing? Did the vandalism to her office have anything to do with last month's desecration of Daniel's grave? A lump of anxiety lodged in her chest.

It had been five years since Daniel's death. Five years of searching for answers and coming up empty. What had recently changed to make someone dig into the past? And Daniel's grave?

The questions intensified the headache pounding at her temples. She didn't believe in coincidence. Daniel's grave, now her office. Were the two events connected? Maybe it was time to re-question some of Daniel's old buddies. Someone had to know something useful.

Her heart squeezed. Five years wasn't nearly long enough to have healed some wounds, though.

Realizing Parker was waiting for her to respond, she said, "I only did a cursory look, but I didn't see anything obvious missing. Perp rifled through all my files, drawers and books. Seemed to be searching for something."

"Interesting." He seemed to be thinking about

something. "I wonder if this was the same guy who searched the station last night."

"What?" She hadn't heard about that.

"Someone searched the station house, concentrating mostly on the K-9 unit and Captain McNeal's office."

"Do you have any idea why? What were they looking for?"

His expression turned cagey. "We think it has something to do with the crime syndicate plaguing Sagebrush. But the station house wasn't broken into per se. The culprit came from within."

Surprised, she widened her eyes. "You think a fellow officer is working for the crime syndicate?"

"That's one theory. Though I can't help but wonder if the two incidents somehow connect to Captain McNeal's missing dog, Rio."

"Last month, K-9 Officer Jackson Worth spotted a masked man clad in black who was walking a dog matching Rio's description. We also have a witness who saw someone dressed like you've described kill a man in cold blood."

A shiver of dread worked its way over Melody's flesh. She was thankful the intruder had decided to just knock her down rather than kill her.

What was he searching for? And would he be back? Maybe this break-in had nothing to do

with her nephew's grave. Or maybe it had everything to do with it.

She intended to find out, regardless of the danger.

At four that afternoon, Parker's captain sum-
moned him to his office. He knocked lightly before opening the door.

Captain Slade McNeal sat at his desk. He held
the file with Parker's notes from the day. "So
tell me what you think about this break-in at the
youth center."

Only four years older than Parker, Slade had
slightly salted dark hair and a square jaw. Lines
of stress bracketed his blue eyes.

Stepping fully into Slade's office, Parker
said, "The perp who broke into the youth center
matches Nicki Johnson's description of the man
who killed Gunther Lamont last month. The CSU
techs didn't find anything useful." Not that he
expected them to. So far the ski-mask guy had
been very careful. No prints, no clear description identifying him.

"Did Detective Zachary find anything missing?"

An image of the pretty dark-haired, blue-eyed
woman rose in Parker's mind. He didn't know
Melody well. She kept pretty much to herself and
devoted most of her free time to the Sagebrush

Youth Center. A supposed alternative to the drug scene for the teens of Sagebrush.

But Parker was dubious of any place where teens with drug habits gathered. Though he appreciated the intention behind the youth center, he just wasn't convinced any place was safe from the invading poison.

Rumor had it that too many kids were partying on the center grounds.

Nothing had ever come of the internal investigation their captain had initiated. But that didn't mean it wasn't happening, which was why Parker and Sherlock had headed over to the center when the news came in that there'd been a break-in. The crime syndicate overrunning Sagebrush had their hands in the drug trade and would no doubt see the youth center as a viable outlet for their product.

Painful memories of his younger brother raced unbidden to the forefront of his mind. A deep sadness welled. Followed quickly by the anger that always chased after thoughts of Ethan.

His brother had died from tainted drugs.

Forcing his own personal torment back to the dark recesses of his mind, he answered, "No, nothing missing. Perp ransacked her office. She has no idea what he was looking for."

Slade narrowed his blue eyes. "The code?"

Parker shrugged, baffled by this turn of events.

"Maybe. But why her office? She's not a part of our unit."

"Assuming that the masked perpetrator and The Boss are the same person, he must be getting desperate," Slade said.

Parker's cell buzzed, and he checked the caller ID. He didn't recognize the number. "Parker Adams."

"You better hustle over to the youth center. There's a drug deal going down."

Parker recognized his confidential informant's gruff voice. "What kind of drugs?"

"How should I know?" The man hung up.

Parker blew out a frustrated breath. Sometimes Harry Trenton was a pain in the neck. But his intel was usually worth the stipend Parker regularly doled out to him. Which meant the youth center wasn't what it seemed. An image of the lovely Melody rose in Parker's mind. He sure hoped the pretty detective wasn't involved in dealing drugs. He didn't like the idea of arresting her. But he would in a heartbeat. Getting drugs off the street was his number-one priority.

Meeting Slade's questioning gaze, Parker said, "My CI claims there's a drug deal going down at the youth center."

Visible tension tightened Slade's jaw. "You didn't find any drugs this morning?"

"No. Sherlock followed a couple of false trails.

Could have been trace amount brought in on a shoe." He hoped that were the case.

McNeal stroked his jaw. "Check it out. If you find something concrete, let me know. I'll have to inform Captain Drexel."

The captain of the homicide division and Melody's direct boss.

"Will do." Parker headed out the back door of the brick one-story building and jogged the short distance to the K-9 Training Center on the adjacent lot. Parker had dropped Sherlock off a little earlier with the training staff because, being a two-year-old beagle, the dog needed some time to run around and burn off his excess energy so he'd be ready to focus when needed.

Callie Peterson, the lead trainer for the Sagebrush Special Operations K-9 Unit, greeted Parker with a smile and a wave as Parker approached the training yard.

"Sherlock's in kennel one," she called out as she worked with Justice, a good-looking bloodhound, and his handler, Austin Black.

"Hey, Parker," Austin called out.

Parker lifted his hand acknowledging his friend and fellow team member.

Continued training for all the dogs of the K-9 unit was mandatory and necessary to keep the dogs and their handlers fresh and working well together. Justice was an integral part of the unit, his specialty search and rescue. Thanks to Austin and Justice, seven-year-old Brady Billows had been found unscathed after two thugs working for The Boss nabbed the boy because he'd been a witness to the assault on Captain McNeal's father and Rio's kidnapping.

Now if they could only find the captain's beloved dog. Even a twenty-five-thousand-dollar reward offered by the captain's good friend, Dante Frears, hadn't yielded any results. Everyone was working hard to bring Rio home.

Going to the kennel door, Parker grabbed the nylon leash from the nearby hook. Sherlock's short legs kicked up dirt as he jumped at the door clearly wanting to be set free.

"Settle down, boy," Parker said softly as he opened the dog-run door.

Instantly, Sherlock sat, his tail thumping the ground, his big brown eyes staring at Parker.

Love for the little beagle filled Parker as he clipped on the leash and led the dog toward his vehicle. "Come on, boy, we've got work to do."

With his lights flashing, Parker drove the few blocks to the youth center with Sherlock inside his special crate mounted in the back passenger area of the SUV. Parker glanced in the rearview mirror at Sherlock. Affection rushed to the surface. The dog was the closest thing to family Parker had in Sagebrush. His parents had moved to San Antonio not long after his kid brother's death.

The sharp pain of loss stabbed at him. Parker's life plan had changed that day. He vowed to keep the streets drug free. A tall order for just one person, but Parker figured for every drug dealer he put behind bars, more kids would have a chance to live.

He'd gone on to the local college, but instead of majoring in business as he'd planned, he'd majored in criminal justice. As soon as he'd graduated, he joined the police academy, setting his sights on becoming a narcotics detective. When he'd been offered the job to work with the K-9 unit, he jumped at the chance. Sherlock was the best drug-sniffing beagle in the whole state of Texas.

They both proudly wore the Sagebrush Police Department emblem.

Parker brought the official K-9 unit vehicle to a halt at the curb, climbed out and opened the back door for Sherlock. The beagle jumped out. Immediately, his nose went to the ground, sniffing for a trail to follow. Reining in the leash, Parker walked toward the front of the Sagebrush Youth Center.

A squeaking sound drew Parker's attention. An old man, dressed in ragged clothing, pushed a shopping cart full of his possessions down the sidewalk. Their gazes met. Surreptitiously, Harry, the confidential informant who'd called Parker, pointed one gnarled finger toward the rear of the building.

Without acknowledging the old man, Parker veered Sherlock away from the front steps and hurried toward the back of the building where a wire fence, erected to keep in stray balls from the basketball hoops, dug into the cement of an old parking lot. Voices echoed off the sides of the center.

"Look, you don't scare me."

Parker recognized Melody's voice. The words were spoken evenly enough but a faint tremor of fear underscored them.

"You should be scared, lady. You're all alone. We can do whatever we want with you."

The pretty detective was in trouble.

TWO

Parker quickened his pace, anxious to help his co-worker before anything bad happened.

"Tell me what you know about Daniel," Melody insisted. "Why was his grave desecrated? What was he into before he died?"

This didn't sound like a drug deal. Parker rounded the corner. A rough-looking character brandishing a knife had Melody backed up against the brick wall.

His stomach muscles tightened. Concern spread through his chest.

Two other equally seedy-looking thugs stood nearby leering at her. Melody's hands were up in a placating way, but she seemed far from cowed. In fact, she looked downright impressive in her tailored pantsuit, crisp white blouse and black boots. Her dark hair was gathered up at the nape of her neck by a gold clip. Truth was, he'd never seen her appear more collected.

She stared at her assailant with hard blue eyes

and pressed her questions. "Was Daniel dealing drugs? You were his friend back then, so you have to know something. What was he doing in the woods the night he died?"

"I'm not telling you nothing," the knife-wielding guy said. To emphasize his point, he stepped closer and pressed the knife to her throat. Melody didn't flinch.

Either the woman was incredibly brave or had a death wish. Parker wasn't going to wait to find out which. He put his hand on the Glock at his side and stepped inside the fence. "Sagebrush PD. Drop your weapon. Back away from the officer."

The two thugs immediately bolted as if their feet had been lit on fire. They ran past Parker and disappeared around the corner of the building. Sherlock barked and pulled at his leash, wanting to give chase. The hoodlum with the knife backed up a step but didn't lower his weapon.

Now that Parker got a better look at him, he realized he knew the young man—Zane Peabody. He'd locked him up a couple of times on drug-possession charges.

Sherlock continued to bark and strain at his leash. He pawed the ground, showing signs of aggression reserved for when he was on the scent of drugs. Parker didn't doubt Sherlock smelled some cocaine or weed or something else illicit on the younger man. Zane was a user. Parker had come here to bust a junkie and his dealer. But that wasn't the situation here. Right now Parker's concern was to ensure his fellow officer's safety.

"Don't be stupid, man," Parker said. "Drop the knife."

Melody scowled at Parker. Then turned back to her assailant. "Zane, come on, talk to me. You guys were friends. Doesn't that mean anything to you?"

Zane wiped at his nose with his free hand. "He's gone. You can't help him now."

"I can find out who killed him," she said.

Parker inched closer, keeping Sherlock at his heels.

Zane backed up more. His gaze darted back and forth between Melody and Parker and then dropped to Sherlock. "If I talk to you I'm as good as dead. Just like Daniel."

"I can protect you," Melody insisted, taking a step forward.

Zane shook his head. "You can't protect me." Fear twisted his features. "The Boss owns these streets. He'll know. He knows everything." He backed up even more. "You better watch out, lady. Asking questions could get you killed." Then he ran.

His words hung in the air. A warning. A threat.

Every protective instinct Parker possessed came to life.

But one look at Melody's determined face made Parker's stomach drop to the heels of his black steel-toed leather uniform boots. The cold-case detective wasn't going to back down, even if that meant putting her life in the crosshairs of the mysterious and brutal crime syndicate.

"Thanks a lot," Melody groused as they watched Zane disappear around the corner. "You scared him off."

Figures she'd go on the attack. He'd heard that she was a tough lady. She'd have to be to deal with teens as much as she did.

"I saved your life," Parker said, falling into step with her as she marched toward a flight of stairs leading to the basement door of the youth center. Sherlock trotted alongside of him, his black nose close to the ground.

"I had it handled."

And he could sing like Sinatra. Not. "That situation could have turned bad in a heartbeat."

She stopped at the top of the stairs and faced him. Her bright blue eyes flashed with indignation. "I wasn't in trouble. And I don't need a white knight to save me. Zane wouldn't have hurt me. He'd been a friend of my nephew's."

Sherlock lay down on the cement, with his

head on his paws. Clearly the dog didn't smell anything worth tracking.

"Familiarity breeds compliancy," Parker commented.

She grimaced. "Cute."

"What do you mean 'had been a friend?'"

Sorrow darkened her expression. "My nephew was Daniel Jones."

A sad case. A cold case. Or was it? Parker had seen the damage done to Daniel Jones's casket last month when it had been forced open and searched. "I hadn't realized you two were related." Empathy wove its way through him. "I'm sorry for your loss."

She nodded, acknowledging his sentiment. "Was there a reason you showed up?"

"I received a tip a drug deal was going down." He braced himself for her reaction.

Her mouth pressed in a firm line as annoyance darkened her eyes. For a long moment she stared at him. "What will it take to convince you the center is legit?" she finally asked.

Good question. One he didn't have an answer for. There was no reason not to believe the pretty detective was all she seemed. Hardworking, dedicated and professional.

Maybe he was letting his own issues cloud his judgment. But that didn't explain why she had a known drug user on the youth center's property.

"What was Zane doing here? And why were you asking him about your nephew?"

Melody sighed and struggled to put her thought process into words. "I reached out to him. I admit it was a long shot, but it occurred to me since Daniel's grave had been defiled last month that maybe the break-in had something to do with his case. Since I have the files and evidence from that night in my office, it made sense."

She sighed and leaned against the railing. "I was hoping Zane would have remembered something or would say something to help me figure out what happened and why Daniel's grave had been tampered with after all this time." Instead she was left with more unanswered questions.

"I'm sure it must be hard not knowing who killed your nephew." Sympathy tinged Parker's voice.

"It is." Stinging sadness swept through her like a cold wind. "It shouldn't have happened. If only something like the youth center had been around when Daniel had been alive, maybe he wouldn't have gotten mixed up in drugs. Maybe he wouldn't have been in the Lost Woods that night."

"I was there the night Daniel Jones was killed," Parker confessed quietly.

She sucked in a sharp breath. She knew that

from the reports, but his statement hadn't been any different than the other officers'. A burst of hope shot through her. Maybe he remembered something he hadn't put in his report. Would he have the answers she sought? "Tell me what you remember. What did you see?"

"Sherlock was on the trail of a scent, leading us through the woods." Hearing his name, the dog rose to his feet, tail wagging, his big brown eyes on Melody. Parker adjusted his grip on the leash. "We found Daniel amped up on drugs and waving a gun around."

Melody tried to picture her nephew out of his mind and out of control, but the only images that came to her were of the quiet kid who always seemed slightly sad. Her heart ached for him.

"Daniel shot at the captain."

She winced. "I'd read that in the reports."

"Captain McNeal put a bullet in the kid's thigh as a means to stop him."

It had been the right move, considering he was firing on the police. What had he been thinking?

"I know the reports said no one saw the shooter. But can you remember anything that might ID him?" Hope swelled, anticipation surged. She wanted to find and arrest the man who'd pulled the trigger.

"No. I never saw him."

Disappointment flooded her veins.

"It happened so fast. Whoever fired was good. We scoured the woods for shell casings. The sniper left nothing behind except the bullet that killed Daniel."

"And there were no prints on the .308 caliber bullet," Melody stated flatly, adding to Parker's assessment that the gunman had been careful.

He shook his head. "Unfortunately not."

Melody's fingers curled. Whoever had done the deed thought they'd gotten away with it, but she wouldn't give up looking for the shooter, or finding out why Daniel was in those woods that night. "I've been working his case since I came on board. I wasn't in Sagebrush at the time. I was a detective for the Austin P.D. But after that night..." She swallowed.

Parker touched her hand. The warmth of his skin spread through her, chasing the cold away.

"Your sister, Sierra Jones, died that night, as well," he recalled gently.

Sierra. A wrenching pain gripped Melody as it did every time she thought about her older sister. "The ME ruled Sierra's death a suicide. She'd purposely overdosed on sleeping pills."

It was still so hard to accept. Her sister had been so full of life, so fiery.

"What about Daniel's father?"

Melody shook her head. "Sierra would never say who he was."

"She didn't know or just didn't want to tell you?"

"I think she knew." It still hurt that her sister wouldn't confide in her. Melody consoled herself with the fact that they were nine years apart in age.

Compassion darkened his brown eyes. "I can't imagine losing both of them in the same night."

"It was devastating. For both my mother and me." As far as Melody was concerned, whoever killed Daniel was just as responsible for driving Sierra to end her life.

His gaze took on a faraway look. "When my brother died I remember thinking how cruel life could be sometimes. How senseless."

Empathy twirled in her chest. He'd lost someone, too. "How did he die?"

His gaze sharpened. "Drugs."

Her heart sank. "Oh, no. Was he an addict?"

"No. He was fourteen and experimenting. The kids he was hanging with were on the edgy side, not overly bad kids but…it only took one time."

She sucked in a sharp breath. "One time?"

"Yes." Bitterness laced his tone. "He'd taken a hit of ecstasy that was bulked up with a lethal dose of MCPP, a pesticide."

She reached out to take his hand, the warm contact comforting. "I'm so sorry."

She didn't know what else to say. His comment about the senselessness of life echoed in her head. She wanted to refute his words, tell him that with God, everything made sense, everything had a purpose, but how could she say that in the face of his brother's pointless and painful death?

Deep inside her, restless doubts stirred.

Lord, increase my faith, her heart whispered as it did every time uncertainty reared its ugly head.

Parker's hand slid over hers, the pressure firm as if he needed to hold on. "So you can see why even the mere hint of drugs sets me off."

"I do understand. I feel the same way. I started the center to honor Daniel's memory. But my hope is to give kids a chance to find happiness without getting high," Melody explained. She had to make him see the importance of the youth center. "We've done good work here. My vision has always been to keep these kids off the street and out of trouble."

"I'm sure your sister would be proud of you," Parker said.

She appreciated his saying so. Now if only he stopped thinking the worst of the center... Maybe if he became more familiar with the center and the teens, he'd see that the rumors about drugs here were unfounded. That they *were* making a difference. "Why don't you and Sherlock come in? The teens are starting to arrive, now that school has let out for the day. Take a look around. Meet the teens. See for yourself that the rumors are untrue."

He seemed to consider her offer and then nodded. "Sounds like a plan."

She led them inside the basement entrance. "When we took over the building, we renovated and turned the basement into a gym. There's a full-size basketball court in here," she said, pushing open the double metal doors to the gym on the right. Several teenage boys were shooting hoops. "Real hardwood floors and regulation-height baskets."

"That must have cost a pretty penny," Parker said as he pressed close to look through the open doorway.

The scent of his aftershave teased her senses. Spicy and tangy, like cinnamon and clove. She breathed in deep, liking the smell. Liking him.

Despite saying earlier she could handle Zane, there'd been a moment or two where she'd experienced qualms about the wisdom of questioning him alone. Even though she hadn't obtained the answers she was looking for, she was grateful Parker had arrived when he did. She'd known the minute Zane had opened his mouth, he was high on some drug. Who knows what he would have done.

Contrition churned in her tummy. "I owe you an apology and a thank-you."

Amusement danced in his dark eyes. "Okay, I'm listening."

He wasn't going to make this easy for her. Served her right.

"I shouldn't have snapped at you earlier," she said. "I know you were only doing your job. I appreciate that you came to my aid."

"You're welcome. And forgiven."

She gave him a grateful smile. She led them out of the gym and down the hall. The beagle's nose was to the ground as he walked a crooked path at the end of his leash.

"The center used to be an office building," she explained. She stopped in front of a set of gender-marked doors. "We have two full locker rooms down here as well, complete with showers."

Sherlock pawed at the door to the boy's locker room. "Mind if we go in?" Parker asked.

"Sure."

They disappeared through the door. A few moments later they re-emerged. Parker's expression had turned pensive. The dog sniffed her boot.

She stepped away. "Everything okay?"

He shrugged. "Not sure. Sherlock lost whatever had him going."

Melody's stomach muscles squeezed. She had a strict policy against any and all contraband.

Any violators would be arrested. If one of the teens had brought drugs into the center, it would only provide more fuel to the rumors circulating about the center. And give Parker more reason to be suspicious of her and the work they did.

"How did you come up with the funds for the center?" he asked.

She started them walking again. "Several patrons gave the center's initial start-up money. The Athertons, Dante Frears, Mayor Hobbs and several other business owners. We hold an annual fund-raiser in the fall for the community and usually raise our operating expenses for most of the year. There are two paid staff members and the rest volunteer their time, so the overhead is manageable."

They took the stairs to the main level. Her office was at the far end near the front door. "This floor has all the classrooms. Jim…you know Officer Jim Wheaton, right?"

Parker nodded. "Yes. I know Jim."

"He teaches woodworking classes. There are also cooking classes and craft classes. We have a game and TV room with all the latest electronic gaming systems. The local high school basketball coach holds clinics on the weekend as well as supervising open gym time." She took a breath. "A local nurse gives a free basic health-care class and a couple of women from the Sagebrush Christian Church lead a teen Bible study twice a week. On Sunday evenings, the youth pastor holds a teen worship night."

"Impressive."

Sherlock started pulling at his leash. Melody raised an eyebrow.

"What is it, boy?" Parker asked and let the leash drop. Sherlock took off with his nose to the ground. He headed straight for the bank of lockers situated against the wall between two classrooms. He started pawing and jumping at the last locker on the left.

Parker's expression darkened. "Can you open this locker?"

She grimaced and gestured to the combination lock hanging from the lock mechanism. "The key to the lock has been missing for…oh, at least six months. And no one seems to know the combination. I keep meaning to have the locksmith come out to rekey it, but haven't. There's nothing in there."

She hoped. But watching the way Sherlock was attacking the locker, a lump of dread dropped to the pit of her tummy. It occurred to her Sherlock hadn't smelled anything in the locker this morning so whatever had him agitated now had been placed in it recently. Not good. Not good at all.

The door next to the lockers pushed open and Jim Wheaton walked out. The heavyset officer's gray eyes narrowed on the dog. "What's going on?"

Beside her, Melody felt Parker stiffen. "Sherlock smells something," Parker said in a neutral tone that belied his physical posture.

"We need to get in this locker," she said, her voice tight with anger.

Jim frowned. "Why? Nobody uses it. Hasn't for months."

Several teens crowded around Jim in the doorway.

Melody's fingers curled with anxiety. "Can you break it open, please?"

Jim sighed heavily. "Yeah. Let me get something." He turned and groused, "Out of my way."

The teens scattered, some stepping into the hall, others moving back into the class.

Jim disappeared back inside the room and reappeared a moment later with a pair of bolt cutters, which he used to cut the lock. The locker door swung open.

Melody gasped. "Oh, no."

She stared at the pile of baggies filled with white powder and recoiled as if a rattlesnake was about to strike.

Someone had a stash of cocaine in the locker. Shock punched her in the gut. Drugs in the youth center. This was her worst nightmare.

She met Parker's gaze. The accusation in his

eyes stung worse than a snake's bite ever could. Did he actually think she had something to do with this?

"I'm shutting you down," he said, his eyes cold, his voice hard. "As of today, this place is off-limits."

THREE

"You don't have the authority to do that," Melody protested.

"I'll get it." Tension tightened Parker's jaw as he stared at the drugs sitting on the shelf in the locker. It figured the youth center would be too good to be true. Guess the rumor mill was correct.

Was Melody dealing drugs out of the center? Disappointment flooded his system, yet he had a hard time reconciling those thoughts with the woman standing next to him. The shock in her eyes, the distress on her face couldn't be an act. Could it?

If she were guilty of dealing drugs through the center, she'd have thought up some excuse to refuse opening the locker. But there'd been no excuses, no hesitation.

He'd give her the benefit of the doubt. For now.

Sherlock jumped up, the nails of his paws

scratching the metal locker, then the beagle let out a series of loud barks.

"Good job, boy," Parker said, absently withdrawing a small white towel from the leather pack around his waist. The towel had been scented with various drugs, which helped train the beagle to sniff out a wide variety of illegal substances and was the dog's reward for finding the correct stashes.

Distracted by the toy, Sherlock clamped his teeth around the end and tugged. Holding on to the other end, Parker played tug-of-war as a reward for a job well done.

"Who put this here?" Jim exclaimed, staring into the locker.

"That's what I'd like to know," Parker said, his gaze searching each person in the vicinity. "I want the locker and the bags printed."

Melody nodded her agreement. "Jim, would you call the station and have them send over Rose and Clay?"

Jim grunted his assent and disappeared back inside the classroom.

Pleased with her take-charge attitude, Parker shifted his attention to the kids huddled in a group watching the action unfold with wary expressions. "We'll need to get a court order to have the techs print everyone who's had access to the center."

Frowning, Melody followed his gaze. "Let's take it one step at a time, okay? See what prints the CSU team finds on the baggies and the locker and run them through IAFIS to see if any of the prints pop."

IAFIS—the FBI's Integrated Automatic Fingerprint Identification System—would only show those already in the system.

One way or another Parker would find whoever was using the center as a clearinghouse for their drugs. He wasn't going to let what happened to his brother happen to someone else.

He didn't think Melody was involved. At least he hoped she wasn't because he really liked her. Liked her determination and seeming dedication. She appeared sincere and genuine in her earnest attempt to effect some change in the lives of the kids in Sagebrush. His gaze skipped over her lush dark hair and her beautiful face. In all honesty, he liked a few other things about the detective, too. Sherlock jerked on the towel, bringing him back to his senses. The woman had a locker full of drugs. Now was not the time to be noticing her appeal. He shifted his focus to Sherlock. "Drop it."

The beagle let go of the towel and sat, his tail thumping softly against the floor. Parker put the toy back into his pack, glad for something to do so he could regain control of his emotions.

A young woman with long blond hair came down the hall. When she saw the locker and its contents, her face paled. "Oh, wow. Is that what I think it is?"

Melody took the woman's hand. "It is." To Parker, Melody said, "This is Ally Jensen, my assistant." She turned back to the young woman. "Do you have any idea how that got there or who's been using this locker?"

Ally shook her head. Her gaze darted to the group of kids and back to the locker. "No. No, I don't."

Parker narrowed his gaze on the girl. Could the drugs be hers? "Are you sure?"

Her green eyes shimmered with anxiety. "I'm sure."

The doors at the end of the long corridor opened and the crime-scene techs walked in.

"Called to the youth center twice in one day," Rose Bigsby said as she approached. She pushed up her wire-rimmed glasses with her free hand. "Did you have another break-in?"

Melody grimaced and looked as if she might be sick. "Not a break-in this time." She gestured to the drugs.

Clay whistled through his teeth.

Rose held up a staying hand. "Hold your horses, everyone. With all due respect to Sherlock's awesome track record for sniffing out the real stuff, we need to test it first, especially considering the whos and wherefores around here..." Her gaze slid to Melody. Parker could hear the unspoken thoughts about respecting coworkers. Rose set the duffel bag she carried on the ground and pulled on rubber gloves. "Everyone back up and give me room to work."

She opened her bag and withdrew a vial, then carefully opened a baggie, taking a tiny sample and putting it into the vial. The color the substance turned when mixed with the chemical agent in the vial would determine the type of drug.

"Cocaine," Rose announced, holding up the vial to reveal the purple-colored bottom.

Parker had figured as much. Rose and Clay set to work on fingerprinting the baggies and the locker.

Melody went to the group of kids and talked to them in a low voice. Frowning, Parker walked over.

"If any of you know anything about the drugs, I need you to tell me. You won't get in trouble for telling the truth," Melody said.

Parker's eyebrows rose. Was Melody really that naive to think these kids would reveal anything? If one of them was involved, they certainly wouldn't confess. And they *would* get in trouble.

Was she making this show of trying to find

the culprit to throw suspicion off herself? His gut clenched.

What did he really know about her? She could very well be on the crime syndicate's payroll. Or her partner, Jim, could be. Parker needed to have both officers' finances looked at, see if either of them had money troubles, because that would be the only logical reason why someone like Melody, who was so smart and competent, would ever betray the oath she took to protect and serve.

As much as he hated the directions his thoughts were taking, he needed to report this to his boss.

And her boss.

They were supposed to be on the same team. If Melody had something to hide, then she'd have to pay the price. That thought didn't settle well with him at all.

Melody watched Parker step away to make a call. Tension coiled through her. She needed a plan of action. Get the kids to talk, and then track down the culprit. She would get to the bottom of this situation and prove to Parker the center wasn't being used for drug dealing. This was a one-time incident. It had to be. But the unease in her stomach taunted her.

"I saw John Riviera hanging around that locker," Joy Haversham said, drawing Melody's attention back to the question she'd asked the group of teens gathered in a nervous circle around her.

"Joy!" Tony Roberts made a slicing gesture across his throat.

Melody would be talking to John ASAP. If he were the culprit, then he would pay the price for his bad judgment and illegal activity.

"What? I did," Joy said. The fifteen-year-old girl twirled a brown curl around her finger. "He was standing there, leaning against the lockers last Thursday night."

"Doesn't mean those are John's drugs," Tony countered. "They could be anybody's. This place is easy to get into."

Melody arched an eyebrow. "Oh, really?"

Tony shrugged. At nearly eighteen, the kid was more man than boy. Had he been the one dressed in black this morning?

She eyed the width of his shoulders and decided no, he wasn't the man who'd rammed into her and knocked her against the wall. That man had had broad shoulders as hard as bricks. "What do you mean this place is easy to get into?"

A guilty, sheepish look crossed his face before he carefully masked it with insolence. "The windows in the locker room are never locked."

That was a surprise. Well, they would be from now on. The locker-room windows were at street level since the locker rooms were in the basement. She'd make sure Jim secured them every night.

Parker returned, pocketing his phone. He leveled her with an inscrutable look. "Our captains want us over at the station house as soon as Rose and Clay wrap things up."

"You two can go," Jim volunteered. "I'll stay and keep an eye on the place."

Parker shook his head. "They want to see you, as well."

A flash of annoyance shot through Jim's gray eyes. "I don't know anything about this. I'm just a volunteer."

Melody frowned. Technically, he was her co-director. "Jim, we'll both go. The center is both of our responsibility."

"Yeah, well, I keep telling you these kids are trouble," Jim groused. "Wouldn't surprise me if the captains decided the youth center was too much of a liability."

His words sent a shaft of apprehension sliding straight to her core. Jim knew how much this place meant to her. He and his late wife had taken Melody under their wing when she'd first arrived in town. Jim had tried to talk her out of opening the center.

But she wouldn't be dissuaded. And so he'd stepped up to be her co-director.

She suspected he'd volunteered to help her in order to protect her. But would Jim take this opportunity to help Parker convince the captains to close the youth center doors for good?

She sent up a silent plea for God's protection over the center. They were doing good work here. It would be a shame for everything they'd accomplished and all they could do in the future to end now. There were still so many kids who needed the help, the guidance the center offered. She'd made a promise to herself she'd do all she could to see that teens like Daniel were given every opportunity to choose a path other than drugs.

"I'll keep an eye on things," Ally assured Melody.

Melody wanted to trust Ally. The young woman had been a faithful volunteer from the beginning. They shared the bond of grief. Ally had been Daniel's girlfriend. After that horrible night, Ally had pulled her act together and had been clean ever since. At least Melody believed so. But at the moment, she wasn't sure what to think or who to trust. Someone with access to the center had stored his or her drug contraband in the locker.

"That's okay, Ally. I think it will be best if we close the center for the rest of the evening," Melody said, hating to cancel the classes and programs scheduled for the night. But Parker was right. The place had to be shut down. At least temporarily. "Would you mind posting a note on the doors?"

Ally sighed. "No problem."

Melody caught Parker's gaze. She detected a hint of approval mingled with the surprise in his brown eyes. Her hackles rose. She wasn't doing this for his sake. "Best to close now and sort this out than…"

Let you close us down for good. She let the unspoken words form in her mind.

He nodded as if he'd heard and understood.

Rose put all the bags of cocaine into a large evidence bag. "We'll take all this to the station. There's too much to print to do a good job here."

"I'm done," Clay added. "I got everything I could off the locker."

He and Rose gathered their things and exited the center. Jim followed closely behind.

Melody ushered the teens out the door. Hating to see the disappointment and confusion on the kids' faces, she said, "You all can come back tomorrow."

She could only hope and pray she'd be able to keep that promise. Would God come through for her? She'd find out soon.

"I'll give you a lift to the station," Parker said as he and Sherlock followed her while she locked up.

She shook her head. "I can manage to walk over there by myself."

"I've no doubt you can," Parker said. "But the captains are waiting."

"True." Realizing that it would be quicker to accept the offer of a ride, she followed Parker and Sherlock to the SPD vehicle.

The thick tension between her and Parker made her shoulder muscles tighten. Despite what Parker might think, she knew she'd done a good job with the youth center. And she'd do whatever it took to find who the drugs belonged to. She couldn't allow these kids to be in harm's way.

She rolled her shoulders, trying to release the tightness. Someone had breached the center with their poison.

After arriving at the station house, they went straight to the conference room. An oval table with leather chairs dominated the center. A floor-to-ceiling window stretched across one wall while the far wall was lined with shelves full of procedure books.

Jim was already there as were Rose and Clay. They'd filled the captains in on the situation. Captain Drexel stood by the window. A tall, African-American man in his late forties, he had his hands clasped behind his back as his dark eyes assessed them.

Captain McNeal sat at the table, his piercing

blue eyes no less intense than his colleague's. He waved her and Parker in as Rose and Clay exited. "Any ideas who stashed the drugs?" he asked.

Melody shook her head and answered honestly. "No, sir. But the kids did give me a name of someone to question. Another boy that wasn't there tonight."

"It could belong to any one of those teens or even one of the other volunteers who come in," Jim stated. His gaze shifted from Melody to Parker and back to the captain.

The idea that one of the adult volunteers who came to the center to help the kids would be involved with drugs made Melody cringe. "I can't believe that."

"Can't? Or won't?" Parker's voice held a note of cynicism. Sherlock sat at his master's heel. He seemed to be staring at her with the same cynical look as his handler. Great. Now a dog was judging her, too.

"Both," she shot back, resenting his insinuation. She understood where his animosity stemmed from, but it didn't stop her from wishing he had some confidence in her. Though why she felt the need for his approval, she didn't know. She hardly knew the man. His opinion shouldn't matter in the least.

She turned her attention back to her captain

because his opinion did matter. "Sir, I'll make sure it doesn't happen again."

"How do you propose to do that?" Drexel asked, stepping forward until his thighs hit the edge of the table. His sharp gaze speared through her.

Good question. She racked her brain for ideas. Her gaze landed on the bookshelves behind where Captain McNeal sat. "More education. More security measures."

"Like?" Drexel pressed.

Before she could answer, she felt something nudge her ankle. Sherlock had moved closer. His nose pushed at her pant leg, hiking the material up until he could lick her skin. His wet tongue was warm and rough. She lifted her eyes to meet Parker's.

Mild surprise reflected in his chocolate eyes. "He likes you." He gave a slight tug on the leash, bringing the dog back to heel.

An idea formed. "A formal demonstration of how easily drugs can be detected by the police would be a start."

Parker's eyes widened, then a grin tugged at the corners of his mouth and knocked some of the air out of Melody's lungs. Boy, talk about devastating.

"Sherlock and I could do that," he said.

"That takes care of the education part," Mc-Neal conceded.

"We could search the kids as they come in," Jim suggested.

Melody's gaze snapped to Jim in disbelief, then to Captain Drexel. "We can't treat the kids like criminals. That will only drive them away. We'll keep a closer eye on things and manage the facility better."

With a thoughtful expression, Drexel exchanged a glance with McNeal. "Okay. For now. But there can't be a repeat of this incident."

"I'll do everything in my power to see that drugs never make their way through the doors of the teen center again."

"And I hope, Officer Zachary," Drexel intoned with a good dose of censure, "that you will think twice before confronting known drug addicts alone."

"Yes, sir," she assured him with a sidelong glance at Parker. Obviously, he'd informed them of the need to run off Zane and his buddies when he'd called the captain earlier.

"Drug addicts?" Jim interjected harshly. Clearly he was affronted that his partner would act without him. "What's this?"

She slid him a glance. "I was asking Zane Peabody questions about Daniel."

"Your nephew?" He shook his head. "You need to let that go."

Anger bubbled and threatened to explode like a geyser. This was an old argument. He'd made his position clear on her quest to find her nephew's murderer a long time ago. "I can't."

The empathy in Jim's gaze made it clear he thought she was working a lost cause. "You've done everything you can and still haven't been able to solve this crime. You need to accept the fact that you're not going to."

"You don't know that," she shot back, hurt by his lack of faith in her abilities. Captain Drexel had given her permission to work her nephew's case on her own time when she'd hired on with the department. "This case isn't unsolvable. No case is," she said. "It just takes time and effort. It's not a waste."

"Time and effort away from your responsibilities," Jim reminded her with a pointed look.

She gritted her teeth. Meeting her captain's arched eyebrows, she winced. The fact that she'd done some investigating today during working hours was something she was going to have to answer for, she knew, but letting Jim's negativism influence the captain wasn't something she planned to let happen.

"With the exception of today, I've only worked on Daniel's case after my shift."

Captain Drexel held up a hand. "I trust you'll use better judgment from now on."

The gentle chastisement hit its mark. "Yes, sir."

"Good. I understand you closed the youth center for the night," Drexel said.

"Yes, sir." Aware of Parker's gaze on her, she added for his benefit, "Just for the night. It seemed the prudent thing to do given the circumstances."

Her captain nodded. "Agreed. And it will give you time to do a thorough search of the facility to make sure there are no other drugs hidden on the premises."

"We can help with that," Parker spoke up.

Remembering how Sherlock acted at the boys' locker-room door, Melody decided having the supersniffing dog's help would be a good idea. "We'd appreciate the help, Officer Adams."

If there were more stockpiles of drugs in the center, she wanted to know. Parker Adams and his dog, Sherlock, were the best means of uncovering any illegal substances. Even if spending time with the handsome detective and his police dog put her on edge.

"Parker, a word?" Slade said as Melody and Jim filed out of the office. Captain Drexel paced back to the window.

Parker nodded and waited until the others were out of earshot before saying, "Yes, boss?"

"What are your thoughts on the center?"

Aware of Drexel's scrutiny, he replied honestly, "Mixed. I know the center fills a need and provides a safe place for the teens. But finding those drugs leaves me with a bitter taste. Something's going on over there."

"Do you think Officer Zachary is involved?" Drexel asked, his deep voice reverberating through the room.

Remembering how upset she was when they opened the locker gave him hope she wasn't. "I don't think so. But I know not to come to any conclusions without more information."

"And Officer Wheaton?" Slade asked.

"Again, without evidence to the contrary, I have to believe both officers are on the up and up."

The two captains exchanged another look. Drexel gave a slight nod. Slade turned back to Parker. "Given the break-in this morning and now the drugs, I want you to stick close to the center. If something illegal is going on, and if either Officer Zachary or Officer Wheaton is involved, we want to know about it ASAP."

"Yes, sir."

With the captain's backing, he hoped she would accept his protection more easily. Though he had a feeling easy wasn't going to apply when it came to Melody Zachary. The detective seemed to have an independent streak as wide as the Rio Grande.

Parker started to leave but then turned back to ask, "Any word on Rio?"

Distress clouded Slade's blue eyes. "No. Not since Jackson spotted him last month in the Lost Woods."

Fellow K-9 officer Jackson Worth and his dog, Titan, a black Labrador, were the unit's explosive-detection team. They'd been working on another case when Jackson had seen Rio.

"Melody said the man who had broken into her office this morning was wearing a ski mask," Parker said. "From her description it's the same guy Jackson saw in the Lost Woods with that German shepherd."

Unfortunately, the pair had gotten away while the K-9 unit was in the midst of tracking them.

Slade's expression hardened. "All the more reason for you and Sherlock to become a presence at the youth center. If this guy in the black mask returns, I want him taken down."

"Roger that." Anticipation revved through Parker. This creep was a menace to society and needed to be brought to justice.

FOUR

Parker and Sherlock headed back to the center. He found Melody in one of the classrooms opening drawers and cupboards. The overhead lights hit her hair, making the strands gleam. Her slender back was to him. Sherlock gave a little yelp of greeting when he saw her.

She whipped around. Her gaze raked over him, then landed on Sherlock. She arched an eyebrow. "Does he smell something already?"

Parker chuckled. "No. He's saying hello to you."

She blinked. "Oh. Okay."

When she didn't move, he asked, "Would you like to pet him?"

She hesitated, and then tucked her hands behind her back. "No. I'm not much of a dog person."

"Did you have a bad experience with one?" That was usually the case. A badly behaved dog ruined the reputation of all dogs.

She shook her head. "No, it isn't that. I never had a dog growing up. I'm more of a cat person."

He'd never seen a cat earning its keep on the force. To each his own, though. "Shall we get to work?"

"It would be quicker to let your dog do his thing."

Parker took the special white towel from his leather waist pack and dangled it for Sherlock. The dog immediately latched on to one end. For a few minutes Parker played tug-of-war. Then he gave the command, "Drop it."

Sherlock released his end. Parker turned his back to the dog and stuffed the towel into his pack. Then releasing his hold on the leash, he pointed. "Find it."

With an excited bark, Sherlock took off, his nose to the ground.

Parker smiled at Melody's incredulous expression. "He is a smart dog, really."

She laughed softly, her expression relaxing into a smile that lit up her whole face. Their gazes locked. The pleasing sound of her laugh lifted in the air and wrapped around Parker, making him aware of her in a way he hadn't been before. She was a beautiful lady when she wasn't scowling at him or eyeing him like he was the enemy.

He cleared his throat, forcing away the attraction arcing between them. "Come on, let's see what he finds."

Sherlock had disappeared by the time they hit the hall. But his frantic barking led them to another classroom. They entered the woodworking room to find Jim holding a chair with the legs pointed at Sherlock in a self-defense posture.

Sherlock had his teeth bared as he barked angrily, but kept a distance.

"What did you do to him?" Parker demanded, grabbing the leash and looking Sherlock over for signs of injury.

"Me?" Jim sputtered. "I didn't do anything. I was in here minding my own business when that mutt nearly bit me."

Fisting his hands, Parker said, "He doesn't react like this unless provoked."

"Jim, maybe you should go home." Melody rushed to Jim's side. "We'll take care of the search."

"Fine." Jim set the chair down. "I've already searched this room. It's clean."

"Great. Thank you." Melody smiled and put her hand on his arm.

Jim gave her hand a pat before he skirted a wide berth around Sherlock and Parker and escaped out the door. As soon as he disappeared, Sherlock quit barking. His nose went to the ground and he started moving, straining against the leash. Parker let go. Sherlock followed a scent straight to a cabinet. He pawed at the door.

Parker's adrenaline spiked. Melody walked over to the cabinet and flung the doors open. Sherlock sniffed the shelves of tools and lumps of wood, lost interest and moved away.

Parker let out a breath mixed with relief and disappointment. He almost wished Sherlock found something in the room to implicate Wheaton. But Parker also knew how devastating that would be to Melody. The man was her partner, they'd worked together for four years. Whatever his faults, she relied on him. Parker had to respect that.

Over the next hour, they followed Sherlock through the center. There were several false alerts, like at the cabinet in the woodworking room.

"I suspect Sherlock's picking up on minute traces of drugs that were left behind by whoever had stashed the cocaine in the locker."

"We have to find out who it is," Melody said, her voice ringing with determination.

"Agreed."

When the culprit returned, Parker and Sherlock would be ready, even if it meant permanently shutting down the center and hurting Melody.

* * *

"Sherlock, attention!"

At his master's command, the little brown and white beagle jumped to his feet on the hardwood gymnasium floor of the Sagebrush Youth Center. His black nose lifted, his big brown eyes going on alert and his tail raised straight up.

From her place at the back of the room behind the sea of teens gathered to watch Sherlock and Parker's demonstration, Melody heard a couple of teenage girls sigh. A smile tugged at her mouth. The dog was adorable with his floppy ears and short little legs.

But Melody had a feeling, knowing the girls in question, they were most likely sighing and giggling over the dog's equally adorable handler, Parker Adams.

She didn't blame them.

For the past two days, he'd become a regular fixture in the center. Great as a deterrent to any illegal activities, which, any way you cut it, was a good thing for the kids. And, boy, Sherlock was a big hit.

But Parker's presence was wreaking havoc with her concentration.

The man could make even the most jaded of women look twice. With his brown hair swept away from his face, he exuded a warmth and vitality that drew people to him. His kind brown eyes and charming smile melted even the hardest of hearts.

Melody wasn't immune to the guy's appeal.

But getting involved with him in any way other than on a professional level wasn't going to happen.

She wasn't interested in a relationship with him or anyone else. After the disaster of her marriage, she still wasn't ready to try again. The last thing she needed was to have her heart trampled on. Once in a lifetime was enough. She had no intention of putting herself in a position where she could end up hurt and lonely and heartbroken again.

And Parker Adams had heartbreak written all over him.

She'd heard other women in the police department talk about him over the years. Parker was considered one of the town's most sought-after catches. The fact that he didn't date anyone more than a few times made Melody think he liked to play the field.

Being another name in some hunky guy's little black book wasn't one of her ambitions. She had enough on her plate without complicating things by getting emotionally involved.

"Detective Zachary is going to help me with a demonstration."

Hearing her name, Melody snapped back to attention and wheeled out the cart full of items she'd gathered from around the center. Parker held up his hand, indicating for her to stop a few feet away.

"Somewhere within one of the items in the cart is a towel doused with the scent of cocaine," Parker said. "Sherlock is going to locate the towel."

A ripple of unease ran through the teenagers sprawled on the floor watching. Melody's gaze searched the kids' faces, wondering if the anxiety she saw in several of their expressions meant they were carrying some type of the drug on them and were afraid the beagle would head their way.

"Detective Zachary, if you'd scatter the items…" Parker said with a smile.

Nodding, Melody pushed the cart around the basketball court and began dropping various different items on the gym floor. A backpack here, a shoe there, a purse over here, a jacket beneath the basketball hoop. She'd hidden the towel and then washed her hands as Parker had instructed. Though honestly, she hadn't smelled anything on the towel. Parker must have used pure cocaine because usually if cocaine had a scent it was of whatever the drug had been cut with.

When her cart was empty, she moved off to the side.

"Find it," Parker commanded.

Sherlock immediately turned his nose to the ground and moved toward the closest item, sniffed, then moved on. Holding on to the canvas leash attached to the dog's harness, Parker followed, allowing the dog a long lead.

Within moments, Sherlock started pawing and digging at the jacket beneath the basketball hoop. Melody chuckled softly. The dog was spot-on. She'd stuffed the towel down the arm of the jacket.

Parker picked up the coat, fished out the white hand towel and immediately allowed Sherlock to latch on to one end. For a moment they jostled over ownership of the towel. The kids laughed at the dog's obvious enjoyment of the game.

"Drop it," Parker commanded softly. Sherlock released the towel and sat, his tail thumping gently against the floor. Parker stuffed the towel into the black pack at his waist. He turned his attention to the group of kids. "Questions?"

Melody took that as her cue to pick up the items she'd spread out.

The kids knew, just as the dog had, that playtime was over. "Can he smell other drugs?" one of the teens called out.

Parker nodded. "Yes. He's been trained to

detect cannabis, heroin, crack and crystal meth. Sherlock's sense of smell is a hundred thousand times stronger than a human's."

An appropriate murmur of awe swept through the room.

"How did you get him to detect the smell of dope? Did you drug him?" Tony Roberts asked with a smirk, as if he'd said something funny.

"No, stoned dogs aren't very helpful," Parker replied patiently. "Sherlock went through very intense and specialized training to become a narcotics officer. We have a training facility here in Sagebrush with some of the state's best trainers."

"Does he bite?" Misty Quinn asked.

The sixteen-year-old smiled coquettishly at Parker. Melody rolled her eyes as she picked up the last item. Misty flirted with every male she came in contact with, no matter his age. Melody was afraid her need for male attention would be the girl's downfall.

"No. Sherlock's job is to find drugs. Not hurt people."

Parker fielded several other questions from the kids, his patience never wavering. Melody liked that about him. Liked his calm demeanor and the way he focused on each kid, giving them his full attention when addressing them. The same way he was with her.

Every time they talked, he seemed to really

listen, to really take an interest in her thoughts. It made her feel special. Which was ridiculous. There was nothing special about her. He treated everyone courteously.

Finally, it seemed the teens had run out of things to say. Melody set the full cart aside and came to stand beside Parker. "Okay, kids. Please thank Officer Adams and Sherlock for coming to talk to us today."

The teens clapped and started to disperse. Ally and Jim stood by the door with handouts inviting the kids to Friday night's free pizza and movie party.

"Thank you, Parker, that was great. Very informative," Melody said. "I think the kids really learned something."

"I'm glad you thought of this," he said, his gaze direct and friendly. "I should take Sherlock out for a break. Would you like to come with us?"

The thought of getting outside for a bit in the May sunshine sounded wonderful, almost as wonderful as spending more time with Parker. She hesitated. She wasn't sure spending time with him outside of the center was a good idea.

Her sister had always said sometimes you had to take chances even if they seemed risky. Otherwise, life was too boring.

"I'd like that," she finally answered, deciding

there was no risk in going for a walk. "Would you mind if we found a latte to go while we're out?"

"Sounds good to me. We can stop at the Sagebrush Diner."

"Let me grab my purse from my office." She sure could use the fresh air. After all, she'd been cooped up in her office at the station for the majority of the day, going over the case file for Captain McNeal's missing dog, Rio. A new set of eyes, he'd said when he'd handed her the box full of information.

Reading through the notes and witness statements made one thing clear to Melody. Her nephew's death and the kidnapping of the captain's dog had to be connected. A dog matching Rio's description had been spotted near the place where Daniel had died. That couldn't be a coincidence.

Parker and Sherlock followed her to the small office she used when working at the center. She unlocked the door and stepped inside. Her heel slid on a white sheet of paper lying on the carpet.

A strong hand gripped her elbow. "Steady there," Parker said.

The light pressure of his hand sent her senses racing. His other hand caught her around the waist. She leaned against him, inhaling his aftershave, a pleasing scent of spice and man.

She caught his gaze, the warmth in those dark depths made her feel light-headed.

Disconcerted by her reaction to him, she eased out of his hold and bent to pick up the paper. The side facing up was blank. But the other side had writing on it.

As the block letters registered, she released her hold on the sheet of paper as if she'd been zapped with electricity.

The roar of her heartbeat sounded like rapid-fire gunshots in her ears.

"Melody, what's wrong?"

The concern in Parker's voice wrapped around her, taking the edge off the fear spiraling through her system. She pointed to the paper now laying faceup on the floor and managed to read the words aloud.

"Stop snooping where you don't belong or you'll end up in a grave next to your nephew."

A chill chased down Melody's spine. She couldn't believe this was happening. Standing in the doorway of her office, she watched as the crime-scene-unit tech, Rose, bagged the offending note.

Parker stood silent beside Melody with his hawklike eyes focused on her. Weighing her reaction.

She wrapped her arms around her middle to

keep from trembling. She didn't want him to know how upset the note made her.

The ominous message kept flashing through her mind. Someone didn't like her digging into Daniel's murder. After five years of no leads, what had changed to make his murderer nervous now? And why unearth Daniel's grave? Did this have anything to do with the break-in to her office three days ago? To the drugs they'd discovered in the locker? So many questions with no ready answers. Her head felt like it might spin right off.

Rose finished up and left.

"You okay?" Parker asked.

The concern in his voice acted like a poker, making her straighten. She lowered her arms. She would not allow herself to show any weakness. Since she was a woman in a man's world, she had to be as tough, if not tougher, than her male counterparts. "Yes. I'm fine. Thank you."

He frowned. His warm brown eyes searched her face as if trying to put together a puzzle. He'd find out a piece, maybe two, were missing. She tried to keep her expression neutral, but under his intense regard, found herself faltering, wanting to confide in him that, no, she wasn't okay. Hadn't been okay for many years.

It all harkened back to when her father walked out, leaving his two daughters to care for their distraught mother. Melody had lived in a constant state of hyperalertness since that fateful day. Always waiting for the next shoe to drop. And it had, many times over.

Each time leaving her with a gaping wound that took longer and longer to heal.

She dropped her gaze to the beagle at her feet. Sherlock sat at attention, his head up, his ears alert. Leave it to a dog to be the one to sense her anxiety. People, at least most of them, only saw what they wanted to see. If you said you were okay, they believed it.

"Let's go get that cup of coffee," Parker said, placing his hand at her elbow and sending an entirely different sort of shiver racing along her limbs.

Grateful to have a direction, she allowed him to lead her from the office. Beside them, Sherlock's nails clicked on the linoleum as they headed for the exit. Teens filled the classrooms along the corridor.

The smell of a baking confection drifted from the cooking class to her left. A group of teens learning to knit could be seen through the door of the class to her right. The muted whine of a jigsaw blade clearing cedar blocks came from the woodworking room.

Jim and his students regularly made birdhouses and other wood pieces to sell at the Saturday market.

Everyone was going about their business, unaware that Melody's life had been threatened. She sent up a silent prayer that this danger hanging over her head wouldn't touch any of the innocent kids or volunteers who came to the center. The last thing she wanted was for someone to get hurt because of her.

Outside, Melody blinked in the bright May sun. She shrugged off her backpack-style purse, pulled open the sides and rummaged around for her sunglasses. Her hand momentarily closed around the chunky watch at the bottom. Her reminder of the nephew and sister she'd lost.

Grief stabbed at her heart.

She blew out a breath. This happened every time she allowed herself to remember. She released the cheap trinket and snagged her glasses. She put the dark shades on and slipped the backpack into place.

Parker took a pair of mirrored glasses out of his pocket and slid them over his eyes. The effect gave him a dangerous edge.

She caught a glimpse of herself reflected in the mirrored lenses. She looked calm, collected. Chin up, shoulders squared. Professional. Just the way she wanted Parker to see her. She ignored the humid heat ratcheting up her body temperature and making her want to strip off her tailored jacket.

They made their way down Sagebrush Boulevard to the heart of the medium-size metropolis. The town was a buzz of activity on this late afternoon. A mixture of cowboy and trendy, up-and-coming affluence made the dress boutiques, businesses and restaurants appear not only quaint, but also appealing.

Melody had liked the town the moment she'd arrived, despite the tragic circumstances that brought her to Sagebrush from Austin. Though Sierra had moved to Sagebrush a few years after giving birth to Daniel, Melody had never visited. Regret that she hadn't known her older sister better before her suicide lay heavy on Melody's heart. If they'd been closer, maybe Sierra would have turned to Melody with her anguish instead of taking a lethal dose of sleeping pills.

As they arrived at the Sagebrush Diner, Parker paused near an outside table. "Do you mind if we sit outside?"

"Of course not." Even though Sherlock was a police dog, he might not be welcome inside.

Parker tied Sherlock to the leg of a chair.

Putting her hand on the glass door handle, Melody said, "What can I get you?"

In two strides, Parker reached her side and put his hand over hers. A tingling warmth shot up her arm and wrapped around her like a light blanket. "I'm buying. You sit. I'll order."

Retracting her hand, she shook her head. "Not necessary. This isn't a date."

Though the words were true, a small part of her wished this were a date. It had been so long since she'd gone on one, she wasn't sure she'd even remember how to act.

When he grinned, her heart thudded.

"I know. But humor me, okay? Let me be a gentleman and buy you a cup of joe."

Appreciating his chivalry, she relented. "All right. Thank you."

She told him her drink preference and then settled in a chair at the table. It had been an eternity since she'd allowed a man to buy her coffee. Ever since her failed marriage, she hadn't had the stomach to date. Not even for a cup of joe, as Parker put it.

She hadn't been enough to make Roger stay. What made her think she'd be enough for anyone else? Certainly not a man like Parker, who could have his pick of women. Going through the painful exercise of loving and losing again wasn't on her bucket list.

Not that she was thinking, in any way, that she and Parker...

Theirs was a professional relationship. Though it started a bit rocky, it had become more amenable the past few days. She could see why so many of the single females in town thought him a great catch. As long as she wasn't the one doing the catching.

The slight brush of something cold against her ankle startled her. She scooted her chair back, the metal legs scraping on the concrete sidewalk, creating an irritating noise. She bent slightly to see Sherlock had moved closer. He stared at her and she could almost see a caption over his head saying, "What?"

Parker pushed through the glass door with his hip, carrying a tray with both hands. He set the tray on the table and handed her a white porcelain mug full to the brim with frothy cappuccino. He set an equally foam-laden coffee drink in front of the empty chair across from her and then placed two plates with scones on the table.

He set a full bowl of water on the ground for Sherlock. "I wasn't sure if you'd like the lemon poppy seed or the blueberry, so I got both," he said as he took his seat.

"Thanks. Very thoughtful of you. I like both."

He handed her a fork. "Good. Me, too. We'll share, then."

She blinked. "Okay."

A little intimate for a professional relationship, but she could go with the flow.

"Who do you think wrote the note?"

Parker's question settled on her chest like a lead weight. "If I knew, I'd arrest them."

He nodded and forked a chunk of blueberry scone. "Best guess?"

Frustration tapped at her temple. "I don't have a guess."

"Daniel's murderer?"

"Well, obviously."

"Why obviously? Couldn't this be related to something else? Another case you're working on?"

"Maybe. Captain McNeal asked me to look at Rio's case file."

"Okay. That could be it. Though the whole department is searching for Rio, so why single you out?"

A ribbon of unease twisted through Melody. "Why, indeed."

FIVE

Parker gestured with his fork. "Seems like the threat could be coming from whomever left the drugs in the locker."

"True." Using more force than necessary to slice her fork into the scone, Melody tried to contain her frustration. "And like I've told you before—I don't know who the drugs belong to."

"But you have been asking around, right? You've talked to all the teens individually over the past few days."

She hadn't realized he'd noticed. She'd started her interviews with John Riviera, the teen seen hanging around the locker. He'd denied any knowledge of the drugs. As did all the kids. Not that she was surprised by their denials. Who in their right mind would confess without a very compelling reason? She sipped from her coffee. "The syntax of the note doesn't suggest a kid wrote it. It's too…formal."

"Good observation." He sat back, his broad

shoulders canted slightly. "So if not a kid, then…
there are plenty of adults going in and out of the
center."

The thought that someone in a position of authority would abuse his or her power made her
sick to her stomach. "You sound like Jim."

Her partner had been full of suspicions about
everyone at the center lately, not just the kids.

Parker snorted. "I'm just saying, you never
know what's really gone on with anyone. We all
have a persona we want the world to see and it
doesn't always reflect the actual nature of who
we are."

"Too true." She used her public persona con-
stantly to cover the heartache, the grief she
worked hard to keep tapped down inside. Over
the rim of her cup she watched him and wondered if he was really as kind and grounded as
he appeared. What sort of person was Parker
when he wasn't in uniform?

"What are your plans for this weekend?" she
asked, steering the conversation away from the
disturbing note and the many unanswered questions swirling around them.

"I'm heading to a classic car show over in
Odessa on Sunday after church."

"So you're a car buff." And he went to church.
Unaccountably that pleased her. It wasn't like
she was a regular attendee. The few times she'd

made it to the Sagebrush Christian Church, she'd
sat in the back and didn't stay long enough to
mingle when the service ended. To say she and
God had a bit of a strained relationship was an
understatement.

"Big time. I restored a Mustang Shelby GT
350 a few years ago. Now I'm working on a 1965
Sunbeam Tiger."

She could picture the white and blue Mustang. She'd seen it in the police station parking
lot. Though she hadn't realized he owned it. "I
don't know what a Sunbeam Tiger is."

"The Sunbeam Tiger was the first British-
made car to win a Grand Prix race."

For the next half hour, Melody listened to
Parker talk about his car. Hearing the excitement in his voice as he gave her the historic details of the car company made her smile, and his
enthusiasm for cars was endearing. She wondered if he put that much passion in other areas
of his life. She'd already witnessed his devotion
to Sherlock. She doubted the beagle wanted for
anything. Would Parker treat a woman with as
much care and devotion? Was there a woman in
his life? Someone who shared his love of cars
and dogs?

She had no business wondering anything
about Parker's love life seeing how she would
never be a part of it. She forced back the ques-

tions as they cleared their empty mugs and plates and headed back to the youth center.

At the door to the center she stopped. "Thank you for the coffee."

He held the door open. "You're welcome."

Entering the center, she glanced back at him. "You've been here all day. Don't you have to be somewhere?"

He shook his head. "Nope. Sherlock and I will stick around until closing. Then we'll make sure you get home safely."

Surprised, she tucked in her chin. "You don't have to do that. I'm perfectly capable of seeing myself home."

"I know you are," he said, his voice pleasant, his expression neutral. "Still… Someone threatened your life today. I'm not taking any chances with your safety."

His concern was sweet, even if she knew it wasn't warranted. "As sweet as that is, I don't need protection."

He shrugged off her protest. "We're staying."

The adamant tone of his voice grated on her nerves. However, she doubted she'd change his mind. The man seemed to have a stubborn streak as wide as the state of Texas. "Fine. I'll be in my office."

Aware of him following her, she stalked to her office. Taking a deep breath, she hoped there wouldn't be any more surprises inside. All appeared fine as she entered.

She sat at her desk and turned her attention to the case file on Rio's disappearance. Lifting her gaze to Parker, who stood in the doorway, she said, "This case is so baffling. Why would someone steal Rio?"

He leaned against the doorjamb. "That's a question we've all been asking ourselves." He moved inside and closed the door. Sherlock lay down, his head resting on his paws, his eyes on her. "We received intel that Rio was taken to track something valuable in the Lost Woods."

She nodded. "Right." She looked down at the notes in the file. "Pauly Keevers, an informant, had provided that information. The police department has scoured those woods, though."

"True. However, we're still no further with our investigation."

"I can't imagine how hard this is on Captain McNeal and his son." Everyone knew how attached Captain McNeal's son had become to the German shepherd after the boy's mother died two years ago. A car bomb meant for Captain McNeal took his wife's life instead.

"It is hard." Parker looked down at Sherlock. "I don't know what I'd do if anything happened to Sherlock." The dog's ears perked up at hearing his name.

Tenderness squeezed Melody's heart. She had no doubt Parker loved his K-9 partner very much. The dog was more than a tool to be used on the job. Sherlock was Parker's constant companion. A bond as close as any blood relation. All the K-9 unit dogs were beloved, and any loss stung as badly as if they were human. "You two work well together."

"We do. But it takes a lot of training." He gave her a wry smile. "For both of us."

She held his gaze, liking his humble admission. Liking him. Her heart thumped against her breastbone. She dropped her gaze to the file and forced her focus on the case and not on how handsome and appealing she found Parker. "How is Captain McNeal's father?"

When Rio was kidnapped, the thugs responsible had beaten Patrick McNeal senseless. He'd been in a coma for a month before regaining consciousness.

"Doing better. He's up and around, moving slow, though."

Some of the tension in her eased a bit at the news. "That's good to hear. I'm sure recovering from something so horrific would be hard. Especially for a man of his age." Her gaze snagged on a notation written in the margin of the report. "What is the code?"

When Parker didn't immediately answer, she

glanced up. He stared at her with a curious mix of wariness and speculation.

"Is there something in that file about it?"

"A hand-written note," she said.

He strode across the office, rounded the desk and peered over her shoulder. He braced himself with one hand on the desk. His scent wrapped around her, making her acutely aware of his proximity. Her senses ignited. It took effort to point to the words scribbled in black ink and not let her hand shake with the effect of his nearness.

"We're not sure."

"You're working the case, too?"

"We all are."

That made sense. It was their beloved captain's partner missing, after all. She cocked her head and peered up at him. She could see the stubble of his beard on his strong jawline and the well-defined shape of his lips. His warm brown eyes met hers. She could spend all day staring into those chocolate-colored orbs. Worry that she was getting too close, too emotionally involved churned through her. She refocused on the topic. "Care to elaborate on what you do know?"

"We first heard about the code when Adrianna Munson, aka The Serpent, died." His voice dropped to a low tone. "Her dying words were, 'Cousin. Code. Danger.'"

Arianna had owned the posh diner in town,

one that Sierra had sometimes worked at, which was why Melody had started frequenting the place before the diner shut down. Somehow going there every morning had given Melody a sense of connection to her sister.

The police recently discovered that Arianna was a middle-level manager in the crime syndicate invading Sagebrush. A fact Melody was sure Sierra hadn't known.

A few months ago, Arianna—The Serpent— had tried to kill Valerie Salgado, another K-9 officer, after Valerie had witnessed Arianna leaving the scene of a murder. Arianna had been killed in the process of taking her down. "Was Arianna's cousin involved?"

He straightened but didn't move away. "Nicki Johnson isn't involved with the syndicate. Arianna threw her under the bus by telling a syndicate lowlife named Derek Murke that Nicki had the code. Murke tried to kill Nicki to gain the code, but Nicki didn't have it. Officer Salgado and FBI Special Agent Lewis got to her in time. Murke was arrested and taken into custody. He lawyered up and won't talk. So we have no idea what the code refers to."

"But it has something to do with the crime syndicate," Melody said, her mind working to connect the dots. She picked up a pen and fiddled with it to distract herself from Parker's closeness.

His energy hummed through her like a low-voltage current. "If Rio was kidnapped to find something in the Lost Woods, maybe this code has something to do with whatever's in the woods."

"That's what we think. In an effort to protect the citizens of Sagebrush and hoping to expose the villains, Slade sent out a press release stating the K-9 unit was in possession of 'the code,' hoping it would make the crime syndicate back off. Too many people have died trying to obtain it."

"Did the ruse work?"

He hesitated a moment, his expression contemplative.

She arched an eyebrow and twirled the pen again.

Seeming to have made a decision, he said, "We think that's why the police station was searched."

A sick feeling kicked up in the pit of her stomach. "Which supports the theory that the crime syndicate might have one of our own on its payroll."

"Unfortunately." He placed a hand on her shoulder. The pen froze. A hot spurt of molten lava erupted at the point of contact and spread through her. "That's why you have to be very discreet with your investigation."

She hated the idea that someone within their ranks would be working with the crime syndicate. Given that Captain McNeal had handed her the file and Parker had confided in her about the subterfuge, she guessed they didn't suspect her. Which was gratifying. And ratcheted up her determination to help bring Rio home.

A soft knock on the office door drew her attention. "Come in."

Ally Jensen stepped in. Her gaze widened when she saw Parker, her eyes clearly landing on his hand atop her shoulder. "I'm sorry. I didn't realize you were busy...I'll come back."

"No, stay," Parker said. He squeezed Melody's shoulder before moving away. "Come on, Sherlock, let's allow Melody to get some work done." At the door, he paused to say, "What time do you want to leave?"

Aware of Ally's curious glance, Melody said, "Seven."

He nodded and disappeared out the door with Sherlock trailing behind him.

"Are you and *him* going on a date?" Ally asked as soon as they were alone.

A blush worked its way up Melody's neck. "No, nothing like that." But the thought grabbed a hold of her imagination. She shoved it away. "I do not date people I work with," she stated firmly, for her own sake as much as for Ally's.

"Why not?"

"Relationships are messy and complicated enough without adding the pressure of working together to it." Besides, once he decided to move on, as he'd inevitably do because that was what men did, it would make working and living in Sagebrush awkward. She liked her life uncomplicated and peaceful. Or as peaceful as death threats and unsolved murders could be.

"Sounds like an excuse if you ask me," Ally said.

Melody refused to acknowledge any truth in the younger woman's words. "So…what can I do for you, Ally?"

At seven, Parker returned to Melody's office. Her door was open and he stepped inside. Sherlock tugged at the leash wanting to go to her. Funny how much the beagle liked her. Though Parker had to admit there was much to like about the detective. Even though Sherlock's breed was affectionate by nature, the dog didn't seek out others, preferring to stick close or follow a scent. Drug training had made him wary. Or maybe one too many bad guys kept Sherlock suspicious. Maybe like owner, like dog. One relationship gone haywire and he ran for the hills anytime he started to fall for a woman.

Melody sat at her desk poring over what looked like an accounting ledger. Earlier today she'd had her hair clipped back in her usual sleek style. Now her dark tresses were loose and cascaded over her shoulders in a straight, silky sheet. He much preferred it down.

Her face was a study in concentration, her lids lowered slightly over her blue eyes, her mouth pursed just a bit. His gaze snagged on her lips. Lush and full and a pretty shade of natural pink. He'd never seen her wearing too much makeup. Just a light coating of mascara to darken her thick lashes.

She didn't try hard to impress the way some women did.

She didn't need to. She was impressive any way you looked at her. From her professionalism to her earnest desire to make a difference in the lives of the teens of Sagebrush.

He admired her poise under pressure. Though he'd seen the flash of fear in her eyes when she'd read that note this afternoon, she'd quickly pulled herself together. She wasn't about to let anyone get the better of her. Which he'd already seen in action the day she'd faced down Zane and a nasty-looking blade.

The woman had guts. And that was precisely why he wanted to escort her home. If she found herself in a dangerous situation, she wouldn't think twice about plunging in. There would be no retreat. He didn't want her to get hurt. Or… killed.

His need to protect her stemmed from professional courtesy. He couldn't allow there to be any other reason.

He cleared his throat.

Her gaze jerked up, her eyes widening a fraction. "Is it seven already?"

"Yep." Sherlock strained at his restraint when he heard her voice. Parker let go of the leash. The beagle trotted to her side and sat, staring at her.

Melody smiled softly, but didn't reach to pet him. "Hi, there, Sherlock."

Still leery. The best way for her to get over her fear of dogs was more exposure. Parker had no doubt Sherlock would wear her down and she'd end up loving the dog. Just as long as she didn't turn that tender emotion on him. "How soon do you want to leave?"

"Now's perfect." She tidied up her desk. "My car's out back."

"I know." He'd seen her driving the light green VW Beetle, so he knew which was hers. "I parked next to it when I arrived. Sherlock and I will follow you to your place."

They left the youth center and drove across town toward a residential apartment complex flanking the Sagebrush Shopping Center. She led him and Sherlock through the entryway and up two flights of stairs. The building was older with fraying carpets, but it appeared clean. Her apartment was at the end of the hall.

When they approached her apartment door, she froze.

"Melody?"

With her key in hand, she pointed to the lock where there were scratches in the door and on the gold metal.

Parker reached for his weapon. Someone had tried to break into her apartment.

"This is getting to be a regular thing with you," Rose teased lightly as she finished up dusting Melody's apartment door for fingerprints.

"Not something I hope to get used to or want to continue," Melody replied. She hated the sense of violation that crept through her. Her door hadn't been breached, but the feeling of invasion still managed to squeeze her lungs tight.

"No doubt," Rose said, pushing her glasses up with the back of her gloved hand. "You should double bolt this door. Just in case."

"We'll get that done tonight," Parker stated.

Melody's eyebrows shot up. *Oh, really.* He was now making decisions for her?

The crime-scene technician left and Melody turned to look at Parker, ready to tell him to butt out but the words didn't come.

Shadows from the dully lit apartment-complex hallway deepened the contours of his face but couldn't hide his concern. Knowing he worried about her touched something deep inside and made her ire dissolve like ice on a hot sidewalk.

He stood a few paces back, holding Sherlock's leash while the dog sniffed the crack of apartment 4C. The dog was probably attracted to the smell of Mr. Hendrix's gourmet cooking. The widowed older gentleman routinely invited her over to share a meal he'd prepared. She suspected he liked having the company and purposely made larger quantities than needed for one person.

The apartment door across from her apartment opened. Ethan Ryling and his wife, Kenzie, stepped out. Tall with close-cropped hair, Ethan was a pharmacist at the local drugstore while Kenzie, petite with short red hair and a big smile, was a nurse at Sagebrush General Hospital. The couple had moved in not long after Melody. Though Melody didn't know them well, she'd found them pleasant on the occasions that they met in the hall and chatted.

Kenzie rushed to Melody's side and put a hand on her arm. "Is everything okay?"

Not wanting to spook the couple, yet knowing they had a right to know, she answered honestly, "Someone tried to break into my apartment today."

"I knew I should've called the police," Ethan said, his voice rife with self-recrimination.

"When I came home at lunch earlier, I saw a grungy guy at your door. He saw me and made a big show of knocking and then high-tailed it out of here. I didn't think much of it at the time."

"Can you describe this guy?" Parker asked.

"Tall, scraggly hair to his shoulders. He wore ripped jeans and a T-shirt."

Melody met Parker's gaze. The speculation in his brown eyes made her think he'd also come to the conclusion that Zane Peabody had tried to break into her apartment. But why? Did the hoodlum know more than he was telling her? Had he been the one to slide that threatening note under her office door?

"Should we be worried?" Kenzie asked, her green eyes wide. "I mean, do you think it was random? Should we talk to the super about getting some kind of security for the building?"

"That's a good idea," Parker said as he stepped forward.

"Is your dog friendly?" Kenzie asked Parker.

"He is. His name's Sherlock."

Kenzie bent to pet the beagle. Melody wondered if the dog's coat was as soft as it looked. Someday she'd have to work up the courage to see. The dog sat patiently for a moment then walked away, his nose hovering above the ground.

Kenzie stood. "He's so cute."

Melody nodded her agreement. Sherlock, and Parker, were cute. Too cute for comfort. A fact she'd been trying hard to ignore the past few days but was failing miserably. Every time she looked at him her insides turned to mush. Not the best reaction to be having to her coworker.

The couple said goodbye and left.

Alone again with Parker and Sherlock, Melody debated inviting them inside. She couldn't remember what state she'd left the apartment in.

"We should go to the hardware store and get that extra dead bolt," Parker said, drawing her from her thoughts.

"I can do that tomorrow." She didn't need him to take care of her. She was capable of installing a dead bolt on her own.

"I'd rather you didn't wait," he stated, stepping closer. His gaze touched her face like a caress. "Your safety is important."

His words reverberated through her. He sounded like he really meant what he'd said.

Of course he did. He'd care about anyone whose life was in danger. He was a kind and compassionate man. An officer with fierce protective instincts. And she was being ridiculous to think otherwise.

If she were in Parker's shoes she'd be telling herself not to wait, but to get the second dead bolt tonight, too.

"Just don't get used to bossing me around, okay?" Though if she were honest with herself, it felt kind of good to have someone else call the shots.

He held up his hand in mock surrender. "I wouldn't dream of it."

Feeling contrite for snapping at him, she said, "Sorry. I'm used to being the one in charge."

"I'll bet your parents had their hands full with you as a kid."

She stiffened. He didn't know what she'd endured growing up. And now was not the time to enlighten him. "Let's go get that dead bolt."

SIX

Parker followed Melody back to her apartment from the hardware store. As they entered her hallway, the most amazing smell hit him, making his stomach growl with hunger. Garlic and spices. Someone was cooking and it made him aware that he hadn't eaten dinner yet. Neither had Melody. He was about to ask her to dinner when the door to 4C opened and a big burly man stepped into their path, wearing a bright orange apron, smudged with red sauce, over his jeans and T-shirt.

"Ho there, Detective Zachary. How are you this evening?"

Melody stopped to smile at her neighbor. "I'm good, Mr. Hendrix. And you?"

"Good, good." Curiosity gleamed in his hazel eyes as he took in Parker and Sherlock. "Who's this?"

"This is a coworker, Parker Adams. Parker, my neighbor, Stan Hendrix."

Parker offered the man his hand. Stan's grip was firm but not crushing. He looked to be in his mid-sixties, average height and build, with a bushy white mustache and little hair on the top of his head. His girth spoke volumes of his cooking.

"Mr. Hendrix, someone tried to break into my apartment earlier this evening," Melody said.

Concern rippled across the older man's face. "That's not good."

"I wanted you to know so you'd be careful."

Parker appreciated her thoughtfulness toward her neighbor.

Sherlock sniffed at Mr. Hendrix's shoes, then his little pink tongue darted out to taste the top of his left loafer.

"Leave it," Parker admonished the beagle and tugged the dog back.

Mr. Hendrix chuckled. "Guess he likes my pasta sauce. I spilled a bit on the floor. Must have tagged my shoe."

"Mr. Hendrix is a chef by trade," Melody explained.

"Retired," Mr. Hendrix clarified. "Though I have been thinking about opening a new place. I heard that Arianna's Diner has been put on the market."

"I'm sure you'd have a successful restaurant if you decided to dive into the business," Melody said. "I'd frequent the place for sure."

She started for her apartment when Mr. Hendrix asked, "Have you two eaten yet?"

"No, sir," Parker answered. "Whatever you're making smells delicious."

Stan grinned. "Well, then you're in luck. I made an extra batch of manicotti. Hold on a sec," he said, and disappeared inside his apartment.

"Oh, now you've done it," Melody said with mirth dancing in her eyes.

"I didn't mean…" Embarrassed, Parker let the words dangle.

She waved off his dismay. "He loves to show off his cooking."

When Stan returned, he carried a pan of delicious-looking manicotti. Tubular pasta shells stuffed with rich ricotta cheese. The sauce made of spices, tomatoes, basil and garlic. Parker's mouth watered.

"You don't have to do this," Melody protested when he offered her the pan. Though her protest didn't have much vehemence to it. Made Parker think they've been through this routine before.

"I know I don't," he huffed. "But I made way too much."

She kissed his cheek with affection. "Thank you."

He transferred the pot holders and pan to her hands and winked. "Enjoy."

It was obvious Stan thought something was

going on between them. Before Parker could disabuse him of the idea, Mr. Hendrix disappeared back inside his apartment.

Parker noted the slight pink hue to Melody's cheeks and couldn't help being amused and a bit intrigued. He had to admit if he were in the market for a relationship, she'd be an excellent candidate. Smart, pretty, thoughtful and enjoyable company. But he wasn't. His focus was on the job. There was no time or energy to pursue a love life or to risk failing one. Though he could be a friend to Melody.

Friends didn't put unobtainable expectations on each other, which seemed to be part and parcel of romantic relationships.

"Does he often offer you food?" Parker asked, taking the key from her hand and unlocking her apartment door.

"Usually he invites me in to eat with him," she replied as she moved past him and entered her apartment. She went straight to the kitchen bar and set the pan of manicotti down.

Parker closed the door and looked around. The apartment was small, but comfortable. And surprisingly feminine. With her tailored suits, sleek hair and minimal makeup, he'd expected a more austere or modern place in maybe a black and white monochromatic scheme or in a neutral palette. Not so.

The walls were painted a light dusty blue, the carpet a thick-cut pile in a soft eggshell. A cozy sitting area was the centerpiece of the living room. Two floral-printed love seats sat across from each other. A glass table between the couches looked weighted down with numerous women's magazines. The built-in cabinetry in a light wood grain was filled with books, trinkets and DVD cases. However, he didn't see a television. Must be in her bedroom. He had to admit he was curious to see what her inner sanctuary was like. Would her private space be flowery and girly, too?

Steering his thoughts from that dangerous land mine, he noted that plants topped every available surface. Large feathery ferns stuffed between rows of books. Fresh roses on a round table by the window. A potted, big leafy plant stood on a stand in the corner. "Nice digs."

"Thank you. It's a work in progress."

She offered him an almost shy smile, which he found charming. He had a feeling she didn't let many people see this side of her. He felt honored and fascinated. There was more to this woman than met the eye. He wanted to know what made her tick. Yet, he was sure delving deeper wouldn't be wise because he might find himself caring for her in ways he shouldn't.

She shrugged off her purse and hung it on a

peg near the refrigerator. He stationed Sherlock by the door. "Down."

The beagle lay obediently.

Parker joined Melody in the kitchen. Oak cabinets and cream-colored tile appeared straight out of the eighties. But touches of whimsy softened the effect. Apparently, Melody had a thing for Disney. There were knickknacks and pictures of various different animated characters scattered throughout the living areas. Including a stuffed version of the Cheshire Cat that sat on top of the refrigerator. Definitely a multifaceted woman. And the more he discovered about her, the more fascinating she became. He'd better be careful or he'd find himself sliding from fascination to affection pretty quickly.

She handed him a bowl of water. "For Sherlock. I don't have any dog food."

The thoughtful gesture touched him deeply. "Thank you. Do you have any carrots?"

With a nod, she fished a bag of baby carrots out of the refrigerator. Parker took a few and set them on the entryway floor alongside the bowl of water. Sherlock went to town on the orange sticks and lapped at the water.

While Melody set out plates and utensils on the bar, Parker's gaze was drawn to the fridge door. Several magnets dotted the surface, holding up various different things. A thank-you note card, a receipt and an invitation he recognized. He had the same invitation sitting on the counter of his own kitchen.

The Founder's Ball was the social event of the year for Sagebrush. Everyone who was anyone in town attended. The whole department was expected to go, except for the lowest ranking least-senior officers. The Founder's Ball was an annual fund-raiser, the money going to a different cause each year. This year the money was going toward a new pediatric wing of the hospital. Was Melody going? If so, with whom? The thought that she'd have a date darkened his mood. Did he dare ask? In the interest of her safety, yeah, he should ask.

"Are you attending the ball on Friday?"

"I didn't know *not* going was an option," she commented as she deftly chopped up lettuce for a salad and scooped the pieces into a bowl.

He chuckled. "It's not." The question burning a hole through his mind popped out. "Are you going with anyone?"

She glanced up at him and then looked quickly away. "No. I'm planning on making an appearance and then scooting out."

"You'll have to stay for the entertainment," he said, without acknowledging how her answer lightened his mood. "I sing in a quartet and we're performing." As if she'd find that an enticement. *Cool it, Adams.*

"You sing?"

His chest puffed up a bit. "I do."

"Interesting." She tossed a handful of baby carrots and cherry tomatoes with the salad. She carried the bowl to the table.

Using the pot holders, he transferred the pan of manicotti to the table, as well.

"Interesting enough to tempt you to stay for the whole shindig?"

"Maybe," she said noncommittally.

"We could go together," he offered, surprised by how much the idea appealed to him. And not just because if she came with him to the event, he'd be able to ensure her safety.

She stilled. "I don't know about that. I don't really think it's a good idea for us to…I mean outside of work…"

The rejection in her words dug into him like the sharp tip of a skewer. Bothered by his reaction as much as by her words, he strove to re-assure her. "We'd be going as friends. Nothing more," he said as much to convince her as to convince himself.

The anxious expression on her face eased a bit. "Oh, I see. I'll have to think on it." She filled two glasses with water and set them at the table. "If you'd like to wash up there's a bathroom down the hall on your left."

Feeling that he'd pushed the subject of the ball as far as she was willing to go for now, he followed her directions. The bathroom was an explosion of sunny yellow—walls, area rugs, towels and curtains. But what caught his attention were the sticky notes covering the edges of the mirror, each with a different scripture written in neat handwriting.

"God is our refuge and strength, an ever-present help in times of trouble," he read softly aloud. *"Delight yourself in the Lord, and He will give you the desires of your heart. For I know the plans I have for you, declares the Lord, plans for good, not evil."*

It pleased him that she had a kindred spirit of faith. He washed his hands and returned to the kitchen to find the table set and the dinner waiting. He took the seat across from her.

"Shall we say grace?" he asked, wondering where she stood in her faith given the scripts stuck to her bathroom mirror.

She inclined her head. "That would be nice."

Pleased she said yes, he bowed his head. "Father, thank You for this food we are about to receive, bless it to our bodies and our bodies to your service. Amen."

"Amen." She offered him a basket full of rolls.

He took one and buttered it. "That was very generous of your neighbor to share his food."

"He likes to cook. I think he's lonely. His wife died about three years ago. Right before he moved into that apartment."

Impressed with her generous heart, he said, "It's kind of you to spend time with him."

"I like to help where I can."

"Like at the center."

"Yes. Like at the center. If I could afford it, I'd quit the department and work full-time at the center. Keep it open during the day. Right now we're only open during the evenings and weekends." She sighed. "Mostly because we can't afford a full-time staff, but also because one of the board-of-directors conditions when we opened was that an officer be present at all times."

"Have you approached the board about paying you full-time to be there, rather than splitting your time with the department?"

"Not formally. Though I think the center's budget could handle it."

"It's a very honorable thing you've done by opening the center."

"Thanks." She dropped her gaze to her plate.

They ate in silence for a moment. Parker's thoughts turned once again to the danger surrounding Melody. Who would be targeting her and why?

"Tell me more about your nephew," he asked. "What was he like before that night?"

Sadness entered her eyes. "I didn't see a lot of him and Sierra. She and Daniel moved to Sagebrush a few years after he was born. And I went off to college."

"So she never married Daniel's father?"

"No. Sierra thought marriage antiquated and not worth the trouble." She let out a dry laugh. "I should have listened."

He frowned, not liking the bitterness in her tone. "Why's that?"

She shook her head. "Sorry. That was... I didn't mean to bring that up."

"You were married once?" Which explained why her last name didn't match her sister's.

"For a brief time." She averted her gaze and took a sip of water.

He had the sense she'd been hurt badly. Divorce did that to people. His heart ached for her. Surprisingly he wanted to push, to delve into what happened. But he didn't. He had his share of old wounds and wouldn't appreciate anyone digging into them.

She met his gaze, her expression shuttered. "I never understood—why Sagebrush? Of all the places she could have moved to. But I think..." She bit her lip and set down her fork. "I think Daniel's father must live here."

"Really? Why do you think that?"

"Sierra lived way beyond her means. She waitressed sometimes at the Sagebrush Diner but not enough to afford her lifestyle."

Turning the information over in his head, he asked, "So...what? You think Daniel's father was providing for them?"

"Or paying her off."

"Blackmail? Maybe the guy is married and liked having a separate family on the side?"

"Except Daniel didn't know until close to his death who his father was, so they weren't playing house on the side."

"How can you be sure?"

"Because Daniel called me a few months before that night and asked me all kinds of questions about his birth, questions about his mother, who she was seeing when she became pregnant. He asked point-blank if I knew who his father was. I told him the truth—I didn't."

"But you think he found out."

"Yes. I received a text from him the day he was killed. He said he'd figured it out and the guy was going to pay."

Parker sat back and stared at her. "Did you tell Slade this?"

"I reported it. Doesn't make a lick of difference, though. Daniel and Sierra took the secret of Daniel's father to the grave with them."

"How did Daniel get mixed up with drugs?"

Her mouth scrunched up. "I wish I knew. The first time he was arrested for possession, I should have pushed Sierra to get him some help. But she shrugged it off, saying he was experimenting."

"Just like my brother," he stated as a knife twisted in his chest.

She reached across the table and covered his hand with her own. "His death must have devastated your family."

He turned his hand over and laced his fingers with hers. It felt so good to have someone to hold on to as he rode the tide of anguished emotions that thoughts of his young brother brought. She understood his grief, his anger. "In so many ways. I wasn't sure my parent's marriage would survive. They both blamed themselves and each other."

"Like you blame yourself," she stated softly.

He fell into her compassionate blue gaze. "Yes."

"Are your parents still together?"

"They are. It was a difficult road to travel but through faith and love they are stronger now. When Dad retired from the company he worked for, he and Mom started traveling, mostly mission trips to third-world countries. I think it helps them to help others."

"I understand."

He knew that she did. The youth center was her way of helping others, just as being a narcotics detective was his way of making a difference. Maybe atonement wouldn't be found in this life, but he prayed God would be pleased with his efforts. And hers.

Drawn to her, he leaned forward, needing to be closer, wanting to be closer. The table butted against his middle, slamming him to reality. This bond he felt, though real, wasn't something he could nourish to full bloom.

Work and romance didn't mix.

The names of couples whose relationship did work tore through his mind, blowing holes through that excuse. Several of the other K-9 officers were either married or engaged.

Okay, maybe it could work. But he wasn't going down that road. He'd traveled that bumpy path once before and ended up scarred for his trouble. He had no intention of reliving that kind of pain again.

He cleared his throat and released her hand. "After we clear these dishes, I'll install the dead bolt."

She blinked. "Sounds like a plan."

Yeah, it did. Everything was perfect. So why was he feeling so off-kilter, as if they had unfinished business?

* * *

Two days later, Melody locked her two dead bolts before heading to the youth center. She was glad Parker had insisted on doing the installation since it turned out to be more complicated than she'd thought it would. He'd had a few tools in the pack he wore at his waist and then he'd borrowed a drill from Mr. Hendrix.

Parker was a man who was always prepared and who always did the right thing.

Which was refreshing for her, since most of the men in her life all seemed to do the wrong thing. Her father, her ex-husband. Daniel. All had made bad choices that left those who loved them hurting.

Would Parker turn out to be the same? She hoped not.

Sharing an enjoyable meal with him had also shifted their interactions into a comfortable, growing friendship. He was easy to talk to, easy to be with. A dangerous combination. But she couldn't deny how nice it was to have someone other than herself to rely on. She'd been on her own for so long…

She'd almost spilled her guts about her failed marriage, just barely managing to hold back. And he'd been polite enough not to push, though she knew he was curious. It was in his eyes every time he looked at her. But she didn't need to burden him with her past. It was enough that they shared the bonds of grief over two young boys with lives cut short by drugs.

She exited her apartment building and walked toward the parking lot where she parked her car. A movement in her peripheral vision snagged her attention. Stopping, she spun to her right in time to see Zane Peabody duck behind a tree. What was he doing? Did his presence here this morning confirm he was the one who'd tried to break into her apartment two nights ago? If so, why?

Drawing her weapon, she yelled, "Zane Peabody, show yourself."

SEVEN

Adrenaline rushed through Melody. She couldn't believe this was happening here at her apartment building. That someone was after her, wanted to kill her. And that someone could be Zane.

Zane dashed from behind the tree and took off down the street, escaping.

Melody chased after him, fueled by a mix of anger and distress. She sped up and rounded the corner. The street in front of her was empty. No sign of Zane. She'd lost him.

Frustration pounded at her temples as she drew to a halt, catching her breath.

There was no sign of him among the cars or the trees lining the street in front of the buildings. Why was Zane hanging around her apartment? What did he hope to accomplish?

A prickling sensation at the back of her neck sent a fresh wave of alarm cascading down her spine. Someone was watching her. But the street was quiet. Not a soul in sight. Not even the birds chirped. Her hand tightened on her sidearm.

She retraced her steps to the front of her apartment building. The feeling of being observed intensified. She glanced over her shoulder. No one was there. A car engine roared. Melody's heart rate accelerated. She whipped around to see a white and blue striped Mustang pull to the curb a few feet away. Parker climbed out from behind the steering wheel. She exhaled a relieved breath. Sherlock stuck his head out of the open back window and gave a long, howling bark of greeting.

Parker strode toward her, a big smile on his handsome face. Her pulse tripped over itself for an entirely different reason. His dark eyes gleamed in the morning sunlight, and his brown hair, still damp from a recent shower, was swept back from his forehead and curled slightly at the ends. A flutter of interest stirred low in her abdomen. She fought the reaction. He wore black snakeskin cowboy boots, dark blue jeans and a light gray suit vest over a black dress shirt open at the collar. The man exuded charisma and self-confidence whether in uniform or out. Which didn't bode well for her peace of mind.

"Morning," he said as he came to a halt at her side.

"What are you doing here?"

"I came to see you, of course."

Of course. Like that made sense. "Seriously."

He tilted his head. "I'm serious. I thought I'd swing by and see what you were up to." His glance raked over her. She resisted the urge to adjust the tailored suit jacket or to make sure her slacks weren't wrinkled. "It's your day off, right?"

Narrowing her gaze on him, she answered, "Yes, it's my day off. How did you know that?"

"I checked the schedule."

Not sure how to feel about his attention, she murmured, "Checking up on me?"

He flashed her a devastating grin. "Kinda."

Okay, now she was really confused. "Why?"

He arched an eyebrow. "Someone threatened your life a few days ago. Just because you're off duty doesn't mean we should take the threat lightly."

She supposed that was true. Or maybe he still thought she was somehow involved with the drugs they found in the center. Or perhaps he was interested in her personally. She dismissed the latter. Though he'd been polite and charming, he'd never indicated his behavior was anything more than a cop doing his job. "I'm headed over to the youth center. Saturdays we open at ten in the morning."

He looked at her hip where her gun rested. "You always carry when you're at the center?"

She arched an eyebrow. "Like you said, just because I'm off duty doesn't mean I shouldn't be armed."

His mouth twisted in a wry smile. "That's not quite what I said, but okay."

"Zane Peabody was watching my building."

Parker's stance changed, turning protective as he searched the area. "What?"

"He's long gone. He ran away when I confronted him."

A fierce frown deepened the small lines around his eyes. "You confronted him? Alone?" He shook his head. "What were you thinking?"

"In case you've forgotten, I'm a police officer. I carry a badge and a weapon."

"I haven't forgotten. But you should have called for backup."

"There wasn't time."

Shaking his head, he gestured toward his car. "I'll drive you to the youth center."

"I thought you were going to a car show this weekend."

"Tomorrow after church." He cocked his head and considered her a moment. "Would you care to join me?"

"Go to a car show?" She couldn't say she was much interested in looking at cars, but the idea of spending the day with Parker away from work sent a thrill of anticipation racing along her limbs.

"Yes, to the car show. And church," Parker confirmed.

Uncertainty filled her. "I'm not sure that's a good idea—"

A loud explosion by the street jolted Melody. Sherlock's frantic barks pierced the air.

Parker reacted swiftly, grabbing her by the waist and practically throwing her to the ground. His big body covered hers. The spicy scent of his aftershave crowded her senses. Heart pumping wildly, Melody tried to breathe through the sudden fear flooding her system.

A car engine turned over. Another loud bang filled the air. This time the sound registered. A tailpipe expelling a shot of exhaust. Not gunfire.

Hot spots burned at every point of contact between her and Parker. Sensations zipped through her. She liked the feeling of his muscular body pressed close. Much more than she should. "Uh, Parker, you can get off me now."

He eased to the side and then helped her to stand as he rose. An old car rambled past, black smoke spewing from the tailpipe.

Melody let out a relieved laugh. "I hope no one caught that on video."

Parker chuckled, a deep rumbling sound. "Me, too. I didn't crush you, did I?"

"Hardly."

He captured her hand. Warmth seeped into her bones. "I'm glad that turned out to be nothing."

Staring at their joined hands, she thought there were some dangers that didn't announce themselves with the force of a bullet. Like finding herself way too attracted to her coworker. She extracted her hand. "I better get going."

"I'm driving you," he stated in a tone that said he wouldn't be swayed otherwise. "And on the way to the youth center we can talk about tomorrow."

He could talk all he wanted. She wasn't going to go. Her reaction moments earlier confirmed one thing. Fraternizing with him outside of the job would be a bad idea all the way around.

Melody couldn't believe Parker had turned her no into a yes, but his constant persuading yesterday had changed her mind without her actually realizing she'd agreed.

Now she sat next to Parker in the fifth pew at Sagebrush Christian Church letting the voices of the congregation rising in song wrap around her like a comfortable, familiar old blanket.

It had been too long since she'd attended a

service. She'd found reasons not to over the past few years, but Parker wouldn't heed her excuses.

The man was way too charming. She'd better watch herself around him, or she'd find herself charmed right into heartache.

She had to wonder, though, why he was so determined she accompany him to church. Was it only because he felt he needed to keep her close to protect her? Or did he think she needed church in her life?

Was he out to save her both physically and spiritually?

She smiled with wry amusement. Her grandfather would have approved. But Parker didn't have to worry. She had accepted Jesus as her savior when she was a young girl. And even though the relationship was strained, she hadn't completely turned her back on God.

A slight breeze came through the open window and ruffled her hair, like fingers teasing her nape. She glanced at Parker. His profile was strong and confident.

Her breath caught for a second.

He turned his head slightly, catching her gaze, and smiled. He sang in a deep baritone that she found herself listening to rather than joining in the singing.

When the hymn concluded, Pastor Eaton stepped to the pulpit. Tall with graying hair and kind eyes, the pastor reminded Melody of her grandfather on her mother's side. They'd lost him years ago to cancer, but Melody still thought fondly of the summers she spent at his ranch in north Texas. Her grandfather, like Pastor Eaton, had been a man of God.

As the pastor read from the book of Isaiah, Melody recognized the passage and remembered her grandfather teaching her from the same verses. She missed those more carefree days with her grandfather and grandmother.

When the service ended, Melody followed Parker out of the church building. He stopped to talk to people, introducing her to those she didn't know as his coworker. A stark reminder that there was nothing personal between them. A vague disquiet lodged itself beneath her breastbone.

They returned to Parker's car where Sherlock sat waiting for them in the backseat with the window down to allow airflow. Parker never went anywhere without his partner.

Once they were on the road heading to Odessa, Parker said, "Thank you for coming with me today."

"You're welcome. Thank you for inviting me." The hairs at the back of her neck stirred as Sherlock's hot breath fanned over her. He had his paws on the back of her seat and his nose close to her ear. She shifted away from him.

"What did you think of the service?" Parker asked.

"It was nice. Pastor Eaton is passionate about God."

"Yes, he is. Did you like the message?"

"I did." She was surprised since she hadn't considered whether she'd enjoy the sermon or not. "It made me think of my grandfather."

He glanced at her. "How so?"

"My grandfather was a minister of a small congregation before he passed on."

"Ah. Now they make sense."

She cocked her head. "What makes sense?"

"The scriptures you have posted all over your bathroom mirror."

A flush of embarrassment heated her cheeks. She'd forgotten about those. Of course he'd seen the Post-it notes when he'd used the sink to wash for dinner. "You didn't mention them the other day."

"I didn't want to pry. Besides, I think it's a good practice. Start and end your day reading scripture."

"That's what my grandfather would say."

The pleased expression on his face made her think of her earlier suspicion. He had thought she needed faith. And in truth, she did. She wanted a deeper faith. She just wasn't sure how to go about it.

"The verse Pastor Eaton taught from today was one of my grandfather's favorites," she said. "'But those who trust in the Lord will find new strength. They will soar high on wings like eagles. They will run and not grow weary. They will walk and not faint,'" she recited, having committed the words to memory so long ago.

"The verse paints a vivid visual," Parker said.

"Yes, it does. Grandfather would say, 'Put those words in your heart, Melody, girl. God will move in your life. He will be there for you always. But first you have to actively trust Him. It won't be enough to say it. You have to act on it.'"

"And do you?" There was a wealth of curiosity in his tone. "Trust God, that is?"

The question dug deep, into places she rarely delved. "I try. When my father deserted us, I took my grief and anger to God." Her throat burned with the anguish of that time in her life. "When Mom slipped into depression, I turned to God again, seeking comfort." Those dark days haunted her dreams still. "Time and again, I've turned to God just like Grandfather instructed." Her fingers curled, her nails digging into her palm. "I've asked a hundred times *why?* Why had someone killed Daniel? Why would Sierra take her own life? Why, why, why?"

Why had her husband, Roger, abandoned her?

"But answers—solace—never came," she said, wincing slightly at the bitter note in her tone. "Only more heartache and more questions."

Still, she tried to hang on to the faith of her grandparents because the seeds of faith had been planted deep.

Some days were harder than others. Today? Today was a good day. She wanted a renewed strength.

"It's not a sin to question God, you know. If you're asking from a sincere and humble heart," Parker said quietly.

She blinked. Her pulse sped up. A flutter of anxiety hit her tummy. Could she honestly say her questions had stemmed from a humble and sincere heart?

"Can I ask why you don't attend church regularly?"

Grateful to be pulled from the direction her thoughts were headed, she slanted Parker a glance. "I usually work the Sunday shift."

But this week, she'd been given two days off in a row. And was spending the time with Parker. She wasn't sure how she felt about that. "Did you have anything to do with me having this weekend off?"

A grin tugged at the corner of his mouth. "Maybe."

Suspicion flared. "Why?"

"You work too much."

She frowned as mild irritation flared. "That's not your call."

He shrugged, totally unrepentant. "No, it isn't. It's Captain Drexel's."

Aghast, she stared at him. "You talked to my captain?"

"He wanted an update on the center. And when he heard about the threatening note…"

"He decided to have you babysit me?" Her fingers curled around the seat-belt strap. She wasn't sure if she was angrier that they thought she was incapable of protecting herself, or that Parker was spending time with her only because he'd been asked to. And why was she taking offense? He was doing his job.

"Not babysit. Protect."

"Right." Just as she'd thought. "Look, Parker, I can take care of myself. I've been doing it my whole life."

He pulled back. "But you don't have to. You're part of the Sagebrush Police Force. We take care of our own."

His words slid through the barrier she'd erected around her heart, piercing her in vulnerable places. He was talking about cops who belonged, not those like her who existed on the fringe. He had no idea what it was like for her. And she couldn't fault him.

"Come on, don't look so down. Spending the day with me and Sherlock isn't that bad, is it?"

Forcing a smile, she admitted, "No, it's not that bad." Not bad at all.

"Good. Now relax."

Right. Easy for him to say. She couldn't relax when she was so acutely aware of him next to her. His vitality vibrated in the air around them. Her senses hummed. Great. How was she going to spend the whole day with him and ignore her attraction to him?

"That was surprisingly fun," Melody said.

Parker nodded in agreement as he drove them back to Sagebrush. Though he wasn't that surprised the day had been pleasurable. He enjoyed spending time with Melody. She was inquisitive and intelligent. Not many women would put up with a whole day of looking at classic cars. "I was impressed by how much you know about muscle cars."

She laughed, the sound soft and pleasing. "My dad was always a car buff. He'd had a 1970 Plymouth Barracuda. He spent a lot of time working on that car. I would sit in the garage with him while he tinkered with it. I hadn't realized how much information I'd absorbed until today."

"Does he still have the car?"

"I don't know. I haven't spoken to him since

right after Sierra died. And it didn't come up in the short phone conversation."

Appalled, he stared at her. "Didn't he come for her funeral?"

Melody gave a dry laugh. "No. He couldn't be bothered."

The hurt and bitterness in her tone made Parker ache for her. "That stinks."

"Yes, well, once he left, he left. No looking back."

Dismayed, he tried to wrap his mind around her words. "You never saw him again? Not even when you got married?"

"Nope." Bitterness laced the word. "For a while Sierra and I received gifts at Christmas and birthdays but that eventually ended." She let out a scornful laugh. "He started a new family. Didn't want to be bothered with the old."

Parker's fingers flexed on the steering wheel as anger at her father ripped through him. He couldn't imagine a father walking away from his children. He knew it happened all the time, but the selfish act still boggled his mind. He would never do that to anyone he loved. One of the many reasons he wasn't prepared to be in a relationship. Families took work, time and energy.

Until he was ready to be one hundred percent in, he'd stay far away from that kind of commitment. He'd let his brother down all those years ago, his parents, too. He didn't ever want to feel that kind of regret and hurt again. "Who gave you away at your wedding, then?"

She turned her face toward the passenger window. "No one. I walked down the aisle alone." She let out a humorless laugh. "Which pretty much sums up how the marriage went."

He glanced at her, hating to see the anguish etched in her profile. "I don't follow."

"I was as alone in my marriage as I am now. Six months after we said our 'I do's', Roger decided he needed to *find himself*." The words seemed torn from her as if she were trying to hold back. "He took off for Europe and never returned. A year later I was served divorce papers."

Heart twisting with empathy, Parker reached over and took her hand, offering what little comfort he could. "You're not alone anymore."

"Thanks," she said softly, but there was no conviction in her tone.

"I mean it. You have the whole Sagebrush P.D. behind you," he said, careful to keep the support general. Though he wanted to say she had him, too, but he didn't dare make any sort of promises that he couldn't keep.

"It's nice of you to say. Other than Jim and Kaitlin Mathers, I don't really spend time out of the office with anyone." Her mouth tipped up at the corner. "Except you, of course."

"Why is that? You've been with the department a long time." Surely by now she'd have developed a network of friends.

"I've been very focused on the youth center and solving Daniel's murder. There hasn't been time for much socializing."

He heard longing in her voice. "Kaitlin's good people." Kaitlin Mathers was one of the K-9 unit's dog trainers. "Friendships take time and effort."

"True." She shrugged. "I'm not good at forming relationships. Or keeping them."

She had to be referring to her ex-husband. "You shouldn't blame yourself for you ex's desertion."

"I try not to. But there must have been something wrong with me to make him leave."

"No." Parker hated that she'd think that. "There's nothing wrong with you. He was an idiot to leave you."

Her grip tightened. "You're kind. You know that?"

"I'm telling the truth."

She looked away. "It's not just that. Even when I lived in Austin, I never really felt like I belonged."

"But you were on the Austin Police Force for a while, right? You must have friends there?"

"Acquaintances," she said. "But I never really

learned how to make connections. Growing up I was so busy caring for my mother, I didn't have anything to give to anyone else."

Sympathy clenched his gut. "Your mother was ill?"

Melody met his gaze. Her blue eyes were shiny as if she was fighting her emotions. "She fell into a despondency after my father left. It was years before she finally came out of it. By then I was an adult."

"I'm sorry. That must have been rough." He swallowed hard. "When my brother died, my parents suffered, but they got help through our church."

"That's good they reached out. My mother wouldn't let anyone help her."

"But she came out of her depression."

Melody nodded. "She did. She's working now for a department store in Austin. She likes to keep herself busy so she can't dwell on the past."

"The past can't be undone. No matter how much we wish we could change things," he said.

"What do you wish you could change?"

"I'd have paid better attention to my brother. Not let him get sucked into trying drugs."

She gave his hand a gentle squeeze.

For the rest of the drive they remained silent. Parker pulled onto the street of Melody's apartment building. Two Sagebrush police cruisers were parked in front, lights flashing.

Beside him, Melody stiffened and agitation radiated off her in waves adding to his own level of concern. He'd barely brought the car to a halt before she was out and running toward the building.

Sherlock let out a howl of protest at her departure.

EIGHT

"Come on, buddy, let's go see what's going on," Parker said as he harnessed the dog. They hurried to where Melody was talking with two patrol officers.

"There's been a break-in," the taller of the two men stated. His badge read Sanders. "You'll have to wait until the CSU team arrives to go inside, ma'am."

"Detective," Melody corrected. "I'm Detective Zachary, homicide. And this is Detective Adams with the K-9 unit."

The younger patrolman nodded to Parker. "I recognize you. What's the K-9 unit's interest here?" The K-9 unit shared the same space as the regular police force.

"Detective Zachary lives in this building," Parker said. "Do you know which apartment was broken into?"

Though he had a suspicion he knew what the answer would be.

"Apartment 4F," Sanders replied.

Melody inhaled a sharp breath. "My apartment."

Sanders blinked. "Oh. Sorry."

"Are there any witnesses?" Parker interjected.

"One of the neighbors. He sustained a minor injury from the perp. A guy in a ski mask."

Melody's gaze met Parker's. The same guy who'd ransacked her office at the youth center. "Could Zane and the ski-mask guy be working together?"

"Worth picking up Zane to find out," Parker said. He turned to the younger patrol officer. "I need you to put out a BOLO for Zane Peabody." They walked toward the cruiser as the crime-scene unit van turned the corner and came to a halt a few feet away. Rose and Clay climbed out. Rose was already shaking her head when she stopped beside Melody.

Melody held up a hand. "Don't say it."

"I wasn't going to say anything, except I'm sure glad to see you in one piece."

Affection for the CSU tech spread through Melody. "Thanks. Someone apparently managed to break into my apartment after all."

They filed inside and headed up to the fourth floor. Mr. Hendrix sat on the floor holding a bag of ice to his forehead. A dark bruise showed beneath the ice.

Melody rushed forward. "Mr. Hendrix. What happened?"

He took her hand with one of his. "I come out of my apartment just in time to get smacked in the face by a guy dressed like a ninja."

Rose inspected the dead bolts. "These have been punched through." She stepped inside. "Melody."

Dread made her sick to her stomach. She walked into her apartment and grimaced. The ransacking was worse than at her office. She hadn't been around this time to stop the masked man from destroying her property. The cushions of her love seats were ripped open. Her plants had been toppled over and potting soil spread across the floor. Her books were pulled from the shelves and scattered haphazardly about. Her many Disney character figurines were smashed to bits. Her gaze shot to the refrigerator, to the empty place where her treasured keepsakes once sat and her heart sank. Shreds of pink and purple material littered the kitchen floor.

The destruction seemed pointless. The feeling of violation stabbed at her worse here than at her office because this was her private space. Her fingers curled into fists.

A hand on her shoulder startled her. Parker

stood beside her with worry in his eyes. "What could he be looking for?"

"I don't know," she answered truthfully. "But I hope he found it."

"You can't stay here," Parker said.

She turned to face him. "I've nowhere else to go."

"A friend's?"

She supposed she could ask Kaitlin. Though she didn't like the idea of intruding on her or putting her in any danger. "I'll go to the Sagebrush Hotel."

"That sounds like a good idea," Parker said. "As soon as Rose is done, pack a bag."

It didn't take long for Rose to finish up and give Melody the go-ahead to start packing.

Her bedroom had been tossed. Her clothes yanked from the drawers and closet and flung onto the floor with little regard. Impotent rage reared. Someone had not only ransacked her place but they'd robbed her of control. And she hated not being in control of her own destiny.

The Sagebrush Hotel had an old-world feel to the place, like stepping into a luxury hotel in Europe rather than southwest Texas. Melody felt strange entering the establishment with Parker at her side, like a couple coming to stay for a vacation when in fact she was hiding from some unknown danger that had thrown her life into chaos.

She had stayed at the Sagebrush Hotel for a few nights when she'd first arrived in town five years ago, right after Sierra and Daniel's deaths. Those days were a blur now. She hadn't stepped foot inside the mammoth hotel since.

Gleaming brass, marble floors and crystal chandeliers set an elegant tone. A large vase filled with exotic and expensive-looking flowers set atop a vast, round marble pedestal dominated the entryway. The hotel looked pretty much the same as she remembered.

Parker had called ahead and secured a room. They picked up the key from the reception desk. The hotel staff didn't blink an eye when they saw Sherlock. Of course the dog had on his police vest with the Sagebrush Police Department emblem.

Her room was the last one to the right on the tenth floor. The suite was airy and lit with low-wattage lamps, casting glowing circles of warmth to dispel the shadows.

Awareness of Parker so close behind her shimmied over her like silk sliding over her skin. The feeling left her a little breathless.

Needing to gain control of her reaction, she walked to the window and gazed out at the sweeping view of Sagebrush at night. Lights twinkled downtown and extended in the distance, then abruptly ended. A vast blackness stretching as far as the eye could see marked the Lost Woods, the thousand-acre forest on the edge of town.

She shivered. Daniel was killed in those woods. Those woods hold the answers. Answers she needed to uncover.

In the reflection of the window, she watched Parker set her suitcase on the floor near the door leading to the bedroom. He straightened and stood watching her. She studied his face, the angles and planes, liking the way his hair fell over his forehead, the way his mouth curved slightly at the corners. The way he made her feel. Protected. Cared for. Special.

Dangerous feelings that confused her heart and her mind.

A flutter hit her tummy when their gazes met. She turned away from the window with a sigh to cover the peculiar way he made her feel, plopped down on the leather couch and into the soft, luxurious cushions. "I'm not sure I can afford to stay here more than one night."

"You'll stay until the threat to your life is neutralized."

"Easy for you to say. It's not your checkbook taking the hit."

"Don't worry about the cost," he said. "The department will pick up the tab."

She arched an eyebrow. "You can't promise that."

"It's already been arranged."

A mix of annoyance and gratitude surged through her. "You think of everything, don't you?"

"It's my job."

Hers, too. Only she wasn't the one calling the shots. She watched him inspect the place, opening doors and cabinets. Peering under the couches, running his hands along the edges of the tables, chairs and around the inside of the lamps. She couldn't help but watch the play of muscles under fabric as he turned and reached, bent and flexed. The room grew warm. She remembered herself and why they were there. "Looking for drugs?" she teased.

"Maybe. Or bombs or snakes or anything that might pose a threat to you."

His words touched her, making her think he was really worried about her well-being. His attention warmed her from the inside. "No one knows I'm here. I'll be fine."

He strode toward her, stopping at the edge of the couch. "With everything that's happened, we can't be sure you're safe."

An arrow of anxiety shot through her. "I wish we knew what this was all about."

"Me, too. Until then, I'm staying with you."

Her heart jolted. The very idea of him remaining in the suite with her, alone, had her mind racing with equal parts anticipation and alarm. She shot to her feet. "No. Absolutely not. It wouldn't be appropriate."

Understanding dawned in his dark eyes. "I suppose you're right."

A vague sense of disappointment coursed through her. "You got that straight. I can take care of myself." With purposeful steps, she headed to the door. "I think we should call it a night."

He snagged a chair from the dining table and carried it to the door. "I'll be right outside the door."

"What?" Disbelief raised her voice an octave. "That's not necessary."

"Yes, it is. I'm not leaving you unprotected."

She couldn't let him sit out in the hall where the other guests would see him and ask questions. "What about Sherlock?"

"I'll kennel him at night at the training center."

Stunned that Parker would be willing to do that, she didn't know what to say. That was beyond the call of duty. Her gaze dropped to the dog sitting at Parker's feet. Sherlock stared back at her, his big, brown eyes adoring. "I can't ask you to do that."

"You're not asking."

Stubborn man. "There has to be a better solution."

He thought for a moment. "Officer Patty Truman."

A vague image of one of the female patrol officers came to mind. "Yes. That would work."

"Good. Tomorrow we'll make the arrangements with her."

Her heart skipped a beat. "And tonight?"

He grinned. "There's an extra blanket and pillow in the closet. I'm sure the hotel can handle Sherlock staying here for one night."

He was staying? Melody's palms started to sweat. She wiped them on her pant leg. Yeah, maybe the hotel could handle the beagle sticking around for the night, but could she handle Parker staying?

He replaced the dining chair and disappeared into the bedroom, returning a moment later with the pillow and blanket in his hand. He dumped them on the leather couch.

For a long moment they stared at each other from across the room. She couldn't deny there was a part of her that was glad he was staying. For protection's sake only, of course. Yet she couldn't get used to having him look out for her, because sooner or later, having him around would be a thing of the past.

Forcing back her agitation and growing attraction, she gave him a sharp nod and bolted for the bedroom. With the locked door separating them, she sat on the bed and planted her hands against her hot cheeks.

How on earth was she supposed to get any rest with him in the next room?

"What do you mean you've been staying at the Sagebrush Hotel? Why?"

"Shhh," Melody hissed to Jim Wheaton. She quickly glanced around to make sure no one was within earshot. Thankfully, the youth center wasn't busy yet. "Someone broke into my apartment last Sunday night."

Jim stopped midstride and faced her. "And you've waited five days to tell me? I'm your partner. I should've been told."

Guilt flooded through her. The thought of telling Jim hadn't crossed her mind. There was no reason for him to know. And the fewer people who knew where she was staying, the better. She was only telling him now because he'd wanted to swing by her apartment on his way to the Founder's Ball tonight and pick her up. "You're right. I should have told you."

"Adams knows though, doesn't he? That's why

he's been dogging your steps all week. And why you've seemed distant."

The accusation in Jim's eyes made her wince. She didn't have to justify herself to him, yet he was her partner and friend. They'd been working together for a long time. She owed him the truth. She told him about the note and then about coming home and finding her apartment ransacked.

"And you told Adams and not me."

"Parker was with me when I got to the apartment."

Jim's eyebrows shot up. "You're dating Adams?"

"No. We're not dating. Captain Drexel asked him to provide some protection, that's all."

"Like I couldn't?" Jim stalked away, his heavy boots ringing through the hall.

Melody hustled to keep up. "Of course you could. It's just the way things worked out. That's all."

"Is he staying there with you?"

Heat crept up her neck. Not now. "No."

"Good. Parker's not good enough for you," he huffed.

She blinked, not sure how to respond. His words were something a father would say. Affection tightened her chest.

"So what did they take?"

The change of subject threw her for a moment.

"Nothing as far as I could tell. I don't own anything of monetary value."

The items she treasured were only special to her because of the memories attached to them. Photos of her family, Daniel's Timex watch, the ring her mother gave her on her sixteenth birthday. The stuffed Cheshire Cat from her father. Her fingers curled with anger at the loss.

Jim pushed open the door to the woodworking room and paused. "I hope if anything else happens you'll come to me."

Pushing back her turbulent emotions, she nodded. "Of course, Jim."

He gave her a dubious look then went inside and shut the door behind him.

Melody blew out a breath, hoping to ease the constriction in her chest. Jim would get over his upset. He couldn't stay mad at her forever. They were partners.

But lately she hadn't confided in Jim the way she used to. The way she recently had with Parker.

With a bit of a start she realized she'd put a lot of trust and faith in Parker.

Guilt slithered through her. For the past two weeks, Parker was the one she went to when she wanted to talk out a thought or bounce around an idea, whether it was a case or something to do with the youth center.

Parker and Sherlock showed up at the hotel every morning to escort her to the station and then would walk to the youth center with her at the end of the day. And then again showed up to take her back to the hotel at night and wouldn't leave until Officer Truman arrived.

During the working day, they'd spent countless hours together searching for Zane. They'd tried all his usual haunts and canvassed the streets. But he'd gone to ground.

Melody hoped it meant the danger had passed, as well. This weekend she wanted to move back into her apartment. But tonight, she had a ball to attend. A quick glance at the clock hanging on the wall said she'd better get a move on. She needed to find Ally and give her some last-minute instructions about closing up.

Melody found Ally in the women's locker room. The young woman sat on the bench, her slim shoulders shaking. Tears streamed down her pretty face.

Concern tore through Melody. "Ally, what's wrong?"

Ally wiped at her tears. "I found this." She held up a yellowed, crumpled sheet of paper.

Curious, she took the note and quickly read the words scrawled across the paper.

Ally,
I love you and know you deserve better than
me. One day soon everything will work out
and I'll be able to take care of you. I hope
you'll always be my girl.
Daniel

Tears pricked Melody's eyes. "Where did you get this?"

"An old purse. I'd forgotten I even had it, until I discovered it in the back of my closet. I started using it." She sniffled and wiped at her nose with the sleeve of her shirt. "I was looking for some change for the vending machine and found that shoved in the bottom of a compartment."

"What do you think he meant, 'everything will work out?'"

Ally shoved her hair away from her face. "I don't know."

Something in the way Ally's eyes shifted clanged an alarm through Melody. "Ally, if you know something about what Daniel was involved in before his death you need to tell. Now."

The younger woman hesitated as if debating whether she should reveal whatever was on her mind.

Melody laid a hand on her arm. "Please, tell me."

"Daniel had gotten mixed up with some nasty people."

"Was he working for The Boss?"

Ally tilted her head. "I don't think so. Daniel was trying to go into business for himself."

A fist-size lump lodged in Melody's gut. "So he *was* dealing drugs."

Ally nodded.

"Why didn't you say anything before now?"

"I didn't want to get in trouble. I knew everyone would think I was involved, too. I wasn't." A fat tear rolled down her cheek. "And I didn't want people thinking any worse of Daniel."

"How was Daniel getting the drugs to sell?"

"He had a partner. I don't know who it was. He wouldn't tell. He wouldn't tell me a lot of things."

"Did he ever mention a code?"

"No." She held out her hand, her eyes on the paper in Melody's hand. "May I keep that?"

Melody laid the love letter into the young woman's palm. "Of course. Ally, it's very important you tell me anything else you know."

Ally stood. "I don't know anything else."

Melody wasn't so sure, but the stubborn jut of the girl's chin told Melody she wasn't getting anything else out of her right now.

Ally had confirmed the suspicion that Daniel

had been dealing drugs. And added a new piece to the puzzle.

Daniel had had a business partner. Who? And had this person been the one to shoot and kill Daniel?

"You are not wearing that!"

Melody held open the door to her suite and stared at the women standing at the threshold.

Front and center was her friend, dog trainer Kaitlin Mathers, wearing a pretty emerald-green gown that heightened the green in her hazel eyes. Her honey-blond hair was loose about her shoulders and a sparkly necklace encircled her slender neck. Flanking Kaitlin on either side were dog trainer Francine Loomis, decked out in a black-and-white striped dress with more ruffles than Melody had ever seen on one person, and Officer Valerie Salgado in a flowing purple floor-length dress that accentuated her creamy skin and red hair.

When Melody had heard the knock on the hotel suite door, she'd expected to find Parker ready to escort her downstairs to the ball and her pulse had responded in a manner she'd come to accept. When she'd opened the door and saw these three women she didn't know what to do. "Excuse me?"

"Can we come in?" Kaitlin asked.

"Why not." Melody stepped back and allowed the trio to enter.

Francine gestured up and down with one pink-tipped finger. "What you have on is not appropriate for tonight."

Melody glanced down at the black tailored pantsuit that she considered her best outfit. It was designer and had cost her a pretty penny. "What's wrong with what I'm wearing?"

"This is a formal affair and you're going with a handsome date." Francine's tone suggested Melody should already know this.

"It's black. Black is formal. And it's not a date." Melody couldn't even believe they were having this conversation. "Where's Parker?"

"Rehearsing with his group," Valerie offered.

"So he asked Charlie's Angels to escort me?"

"Ohhh, Charlie's Angels." Francine pressed her hands together like she were holding a gun, cocked a knee and struck a pose. "I'm the Demi Moore character."

A smile tugged at Melody. "Uh, wasn't her character the villain?"

Francine's expression fell. "Oh. Right."

"If you're not dating Parker then what's going on?" Kaitlin asked.

"Our bosses assigned him the task of keeping me safe."

Worry wrinkled Francine's brow. "From what?"

Melody told them about the break-ins and the threatening note. "I think it has something to do with Daniel's murder and Rio's disappearance."

Anxiety darkened Kaitlin's green eyes. "You'll be careful, right?"

Touched by her concern, Melody squeezed her friend's hand. "Yes. Of course."

"Well, if you have to have someone watching your back, Parker's a good candidate. And cute, too," Francine remarked.

"Parker feels protective toward you," Kaitlin said.

Valerie's smile reminded Melody of the Cheshire Cat. "I don't think it's only his protective instincts."

Melody narrowed her gaze. "Why do you say that?"

"Woman's intuition."

Right. A nervous flutter hit her tummy. What had Parker said to give Valerie that impression?

Melody grabbed her purse from the sideboard table in the entryway. "Let's go."

The three women exchanged glances and didn't budge.

"What?" Melody arched an eyebrow.

Kaitlin smiled. "Honey, wouldn't you rather put on a dress?"

"I don't own a dress." Her closet was full of pantsuits and button-down poplin shirts. She did have a couple pairs of jeans and some T-shirts for her days off.

"We can remedy that." Kaitlin considered her for a moment before walking to the phone sitting on a table beside the leather couch. Kaitlin dialed the concierge and asked for the hotel's boutique. "How late are you open? Oh, good. I have an emergency. Do you have anything formal in a size…?" Kaitlin's hazel eyes grazed over Melody. "…six? And shoes?" Kaitlin cupped the receiver to say, "What size shoe do you wear?"

Bemusement prompted an answer. "Eight."

Kaitlin repeated that into the phone. "Good. Pull everything you have. We'll be right down."

Melody glanced at the clock. "The ball starts in a half hour."

Kaitlin waved away her concern. "That's plenty of time." She tucked her arm through Melody's. "Let's go, Cinderella. Time to get ready for the ball."

It wasn't Charlie's Angels who'd come to visit but three fairy godmothers. Melody laughed at the irony and followed them out the door. At least she would be well protected with her entourage.

NINE

"That is perfect," Valerie declared when Melody stepped out of the dressing room wearing one of the many dresses that Maggie, the manager of the hotel's chic boutique, had pulled out for her to try on.

Melody could hardly believe she was staring at herself in the mirror. The reflection looked more like a storybook princess than a cop. She fought the urge to twirl. The silky blue sleeveless dress clung to her curves, making her look sleek and svelte. And daring silver heels with peek-a-boo toe cutouts flashed from beneath the hem of the dress. The neckline was modest, yet she felt like she was exposing way more of herself than she was comfortable with. But how often did a girl get to be Cinderella?

Kaitlin came up behind her and unclipped the barrette at her nape, then fluffed her dark hair around her shoulders. "We'll run over to the hair salon and add a few curls with the hot iron and you'll be set."

"I don't know that we'll have time," Melody said. "Parker will be wondering where we are."

"The man will wait. Besides, once he sees you, he'll think the extra few minutes worth it," Francine predicted.

A spurt of anticipation and anxiety made Melody's heart pound. "This is not me."

"It *is* you," Kaitlin insisted. "The blue in the dress makes your eyes almost translucent."

She couldn't argue with that. Even though blue eyes were a family trait, her eyes looked especially bright right now. It had to be the shop's lighting and not the excitement bubbling up from deep within. She smoothed a hand down the sleek lines of the dress. She felt sophisticated and feminine and pretty. What would Parker think? Why did she care?

Maggie stepped up with a mascara wand in one hand and a dark eyeliner pencil in the other. Nearing fifty, the fashionable woman looked like she could be in a magazine rather than tending shop in Sagebrush. "Let me darken your lashes."

Melody held still as Maggie applied the mascara and then the liner.

"A little lipstick," Maggie said as she stroked a tube of a velvety color over Melody's lips. "And a touch of gold." She snapped open a black case with a variety of eye shadows. Using the small brush she dusted a shimmering gold powder over her lids. When she stepped back, Melody was able to see the effect.

A nervous laugh escaped. The gold shadow and dark liner emphasized her eyes. The red lipstick stood out in stark contrast to her light skin.

She hardly recognized herself. "I don't know... I feel like I'm playing dress up in my mother's clothes." Though honestly, she couldn't remember her mother wearing anything as glamorous.

Valerie tsked. "You're just not used to it. You are absolutely beautiful and you're going to knock the socks off Parker Adams."

Melody couldn't deny the heady anticipation of seeing Parker's reaction. Not that what he thought mattered in the grand scheme of things. Tomorrow this sparkly version of herself would be tucked away as a nice memory. Nothing more.

But she planned to enjoy tonight.

When Melody walked sedately through the hotel's lobby, Parker did a double take. His core ignited in a burst of flames. He forgave her tardiness in a quick heartbeat. "Wow. You're...uh, hmm..."

He already thought she was a knockout. Now she'd transformed into a vibrant butterfly. Her dark hair curled around her shoulders. Her flawless skin provided the perfect backdrop for the carefully applied makeup that enhanced her features. The dress, well, the dress showed off her figure to perfection, leaving him tongue-tied.

The shy smile and the uncertainty in her vivid blue eyes touched something deep inside, making him want to pull her into his embrace and show her how gorgeous she really was, with or without the accoutrements.

He jammed his hands into the pockets of his tux. "You're beautiful."

"Thank you," she murmured, her gaze ducking slightly. "I feel a bit awkward. I'm not used to wearing..." She gestured toward herself.

"It suits you," he said and grimaced at the lame words.

She arched an eyebrow. "Better than my suits?"

He chuckled. "I think you're beautiful no matter what you're wearing."

Her eyes widened. "Really?"

"Yes, really." And the less he said on that subject, the better. Determined to keep his attraction to her on a short leash, he held out his arm. "Ready?"

She glided forward and took his arm. "As ready as Kaitlin, Valerie and Francine could make me."

"Ah, you had not one but three fairy godmothers. That's appropriate considering your penchant for all things Disney."

A rueful laugh escaped her ruby lips. "You noticed that?"

"Hard not to." He steered her toward the elevators. "I especially liked the huge Cheshire Cat." Belatedly, he remembered the cat had been ripped to shreds during the break-in.

Her smile faltered. "My father gave that to me when I was eight. He'd taken Sierra and me to Disneyland. Those were the best five days of my life." She bit her lower lip for a moment. Sudden tears glistened in her eyes. "Two weeks later, he left us."

A fist grabbed Parker's heart and squeezed. "I'm sorry for bringing it up."

"Nothing for you to be sorry about." She blinked rapidly. "It makes me so mad when I think about someone breaking into my apartment and ruining everything. And for what? Nothing."

He pulled her into an alcove and gathered her close. "You have your memories. Those can't be destroyed."

She laid her cheek against his tux and rested her arms lightly around his waist. "Thank you," she whispered.

The fresh clean scent of her hair teased his senses. She felt warm and pliant in his embrace. His chest filled with tender emotions that both scared and thrilled him. Getting attached to her wasn't part of his assignment. He should let her go, should set her away, but he couldn't bring himself to break the contact. He liked holding her. More than he should, more than was wise.

She lifted her head and leaned back to look up at him. The fire in her eyes caught his breath. Blue fire. The hottest flame. Apparently, she wasn't immune to the attraction flaring between them. The intoxicating thought swirled through him. Her gaze searched his face, lingered on his mouth then lifted back to his eyes. Her lips parted. The yearning to lower his mouth to hers exploded within him. Pressure built in his blood. He tightened his hold as his resistance floundered.

"We should probably go," she said softly.

"Probably." But he didn't want to leave the privacy of the alcove. Or to let her go. He wanted to explore the look in her eyes, to feel her body pressed close, to lose himself in the wonder of Melody.

"Parker?"

The slight tremble in her voice slammed into him, forcing reality to the forefront of his mind. As attracted to Melody as he was, kissing her wasn't part of his plan. Or part of his job. He had let her sorrow and his attraction to her muddle his objective. He needed to stay professional, keep their relationship strictly business. For her sake. As well as his own.

Blowing out a condensed breath, he released her and stepped back. Parker reined in his emotions and vowed to keep a physical distance from his very beautiful and very tempting coworker.

As they left the alcove, Melody visibly tensed. She slowed and looked around.

Concern arced through him. "What is it?"

"I don't know." She tugged on her bottom lip with her even white teeth. "It felt like someone was watching us." She gave a shaky laugh. "Probably just my nerves."

Or her instincts.

Forget keeping a distance.

He couldn't forget someone out there had threatened Melody's life and trashed her apartment. Her life was in danger. And it was up to him to protect her. Even if he'd rather be kissing her.

Parker guided Melody toward the elevator. His hand, placed at the small of her back, created sparks of warmth to spread through her much like his words had. When he'd said she was beautiful, she'd believed him. And that made her feel…beautiful. She couldn't remember the last time she'd felt like this.

Several other elegantly dressed partygoers

crowded inside the small compartment with them, forcing Melody to step back against Parker's broad chest. He slid an arm around her waist, making her a bit weak in the knees. Ever since that moment when she'd thought he was going to kiss her, her whole being hummed with anticipation.

The close quarters in the elevator only heightened the energy racing through her.

When they stepped out of the elevator, she expected Parker to move away from her, but to her surprise, he didn't. He kept his arm around her, molding her to his side, his hand resting lightly at her hip. The possessive gesture made her feel cherished. Something she could honestly say she'd never experienced. The crush of people forced them even closer. Heat coming off him made her head swim. Overwhelmed by his nearness, she had to concentrate to put one foot in front of the other.

They jostled their way into the grand ballroom and paused inside the entryway. The opulence of the elegant Victorian-inspired space stole Melody's breath. A large ornate brass chandelier hung from a high vaulted ceiling. Hardwood floors, polished to a radiant shine, stretched across the length of the long room. Grandiose gold-framed mirrors and exquisite artwork enhanced the solid walls to the left while to the right floor-to-ceiling windows allowed the fading evening sun to stream through like beacons from heaven. Above the main floor of the ballroom, suspended balconies provided perfect places for guests to observe those below. A stage set with a band sat at the far end, while long tables filled with appetizers and desserts lined the far wall.

"Wow, this is amazing," she breathed out, feeling like she was indeed Cinderella stepping into her first ball.

"It's lavish, that's for sure," Parker murmured. "I've heard that Dante Frears is part owner of this place."

"Didn't he and Captain McNeal serve in the military together?"

"Yes. They go way back. In fact, Dante put up the reward money of twenty-five thousand dollars for any information on Rio. Fat lot of good it did."

"You'd think a carrot like that would entice someone to come forward with information." Another missing piece to this already-puzzling case.

"Exactly. But I think people are more scared of The Boss than they are desperate for money."

"Which says a lot about the power and scope of this crime lord." Melody suppressed a shiver. Somehow she'd drawn this mysterious criminal's attention even before she started asking questions about Rio.

Ally Jensen's words rose to the surface of her mind. Melody tugged Parker out of the throng of people into a more secluded spot. "I forgot to tell you something. Ally confessed to me today that Daniel was indeed selling drugs. And he had a partner."

Parker frowned, his fingers restless on her hip. "Who?"

"She didn't know. But I'm thinking this partner could be the one who killed Daniel. Maybe it was Zane."

"Doesn't seem likely. Whoever took that shot was a skilled marksman and highly trained."

That didn't sound like Zane.

Parker raised his free hand in greeting to someone walking by. "Come on, let's join the others."

She followed his gaze to a large round table near a window. She recognized several of the K-9 officers. Her three fairy godmothers were also at the table. Kaitlin arched an eyebrow. Heat infused Melody's cheeks for having been caught touching Parker in a very un-coworker way. *Great.*

Melody and Parker made their way through the swarm of people to join them.

Introductions were made around the table.

Though Melody had seen most of the officers and had on occasion interacted with a few, she was glad to formally meet them.

"This is Nicki Johnson, uh, I mean Worth," Parker said as a blonde woman rose to shake her hand.

Melody had heard that K-9 officer and explosives expert Jackson Worth had recently married. Melody smiled at his new wife. The pretty blonde wore a red, empire-waist gown and had a lovely smile. Melody noted the evident roundness of her belly but was too polite to ask if she were expecting.

"Nice to meet you and yes," Nicki put a hand on her protruding tummy, obviously seeing the question in Melody's eyes. "I'm pregnant."

Melody appreciated the woman's directness. "Nice to meet you, too. And congratulations."

Nicki beamed as she looked at her new husband. "We're happy."

The dark-haired Jackson Worth looked at his new wife with tenderness and love. "Yes, we are."

Melody wondered what it would be like to feel that kind of love. To be cherished and protected, not only physically, but emotionally. To have someone put her welfare ahead of their own needs or wants.

A cynical voice in her head claimed that kind

of selfless love didn't exist. That these people were kidding themselves. Melody had only to look at her dad and her ex-husband to see prime examples of selfishness at its worst. Both had left behind the people they'd professed to love, leaving her alone and abandoned.

But a small, gentle voice nudged her with the knowledge that God intended for humans to love sacrificially, unconditionally.

Melody sent a quick, silent prayer that Jackson and Nicki had found that kind of God-ordained love.

Yearning to find that sort of love swelled, but Melody quickly squelched the tide. She'd risked her heart once. And had it sliced to ribbons. Love wasn't a risk she was willing to take again.

The man at Valerie's side rose and extended his hand. "Special Agent Trevor Lewis."

Shifting her attention to the dark-haired man, she shook his hand. "Agent Lewis, nice to meet you. I'm surprised you're still in town. Has a new case come up?"

"He's with me," Valerie spoke up, placing her hand on his muscular arm.

Light glinted off the diamond solitaire on her ring finger.

"I see. Congratulations."

Valerie and Agent Lewis had recently worked together on a case to bring down a fugitive that turned out to be another cog in the Sagebrush crime syndicate. And obviously fell in love in the process. Melody was happy for the couple. She cut off the twinge of envy trying to take root.

"Where's Lee?" Parker asked as he held out a chair for Melody to take a seat.

Lee Calloway was another member of the K-9 unit.

"He and Lucy are in the buffet line," Valerie answered.

Melody remembered Lucy's story from the files she'd read relating to Rio's disappearance. Lucy had been found in the Lost Woods a few months back with no memory of who she was or how she'd come to be in the woods. At first the police had thought she was involved in Rio's kidnapping. But eventually they discovered she'd been running from her abusive ex-husband. The man had tried to hurt Lucy but Lee apprehended him before he could do her any harm.

Trevor held out his hand to his fiancée. "I'm ready for some food, too."

Taking his hand, Valerie rose and followed him to the buffet tables.

"Are you hungry yet?" Parker asked Melody.

They way he looked at her with such care made her stomach clench. She shook her head. "But I would love something cold to drink."

He smiled and then looked at the others. "Anyone else?"

"I would love lemonade," Kaitlin replied.

Francine held up her glass. "I'm good."

"I'll be right back," Parker said and strode toward the beverage table.

Melody watched him walking away, feeling suddenly bereft. Which really didn't make any sense.

Kaitlin scooted closer with a curious gleam in her pretty eyes. "You and Parker make an adorable couple."

A heated flush swept up her neck. The thought of them as a couple pleased her more than she'd care to admit. "I've already told you it's not like that."

"It looked just like that when you two were getting cozy in the alcove downstairs," Francine piped in.

"You're the envy of every single woman here tonight," Kaitlin teased.

Melody's gaze drifted to Parker. He stood talking now with Austin Black, another K-9 detective, and their captain, Slade McNeal.

"We're just friends."

"Really?"

The doubt in Kaitlin's voice set Melody's teeth on edge. She really didn't want to entertain the fantasy that there could be more between her and Parker but her friend's reluctance to believe her was making it harder to block. "Yes. Really."

"He's a good man," Kaitlin stated. "You could do a lot worse."

She had no doubt about that. "We work together."

"There's no law that says you can't find love in the workplace," Francine said.

Melody shook her head. "Give it a rest."

"Give what a rest?" Parker asked from behind her shoulder.

She twisted to see him. He held two tall glasses of lemonade, and she reached for one of the drinks. "Thank you."

"Kaitlin."

"Thank you." Kaitlin took the glass he offered.

Parker took his seat. "So what are we talking about?"

"Oh, this and that," Francine said with a big grin.

Kaitlin snickered.

Melody sipped from her lemonade, hoping the cool liquid would soothe her burning cheeks.

Trevor and Valerie returned, their plates piled with savory treats.

"Valerie tells me you run the youth center," Trevor said as he settled into his chair.

"I do, along with Jim Wheaton." Only too

happy to discuss the center, Melody told them about their programs and services.

"Melody has done an awesome job of providing the kids a safe and healthy environment," Parker added.

Pleased by his words, Melody smiled at him with gratitude. He stretched his arm across the back of her chair. His fingers drew lazy circles over the bare skin of her shoulder, making her forget people surrounded them. She lost herself in the chocolate depths of his eyes.

"Mind if I join you all?" Slade McNeal asked, standing near Kaitlin's right shoulder.

Pulled from the magnetic draw of Parker's gaze, Melody noticed that Kaitlin straightened but didn't glance up at the newcomer. Instead, her friend studiously sipped from her glass. Interesting.

Melody rose. "Here, sir. You can have my seat."

Kaitlin's gaze snapped to hers then quickly lowered. Was that panic in her green eyes? Doubly interesting.

Parker pulled Melody's chair out so she could move away from the table. He gave her a quizzical look.

"How about those buffet tables…" she said airily.

Parker held out his arm. "This way."

As they walked away from the table, Melody

glanced back over her shoulder. Slade slid into the seat next to Kaitlin. Melody wondered why Kaitlin had seemed so nervous about Slade joining their table. Was there something going on with those two?

Parker led her to the food line. As they waited, they chatted with the older couple in front of them. Melody introduced Parker to one of the youth center's donors.

"This is such a lovely venue," Mrs. Atherton gushed. The Athertons were one of Sagebrush's more affluent families. "I'm so glad the committee decided to have a formal ball rather than a picnic in the park."

"I've always enjoyed the community picnic each year," Melody said politely, thinking how the picnic involved not only the adults but the kids of the community, as well.

"Yes, they are fun and all. But sometimes change is good. There was much debate about the venue for this year's fund-raiser. But Mr. Frears offered this place free."

"Are you on the committee?" Parker asked.

"My wife is on all the committees," Mr. Atherton intoned with a good dose of humor.

"I like to be involved," Mrs. Atherton huffed.

"More like you want to be in control, dear," her husband teased with a light laugh as he took a plate from a high stack.

"Nonsense." Mrs. Atherton touched the string of pearls at her neck.

Mr. Atherton winked at them before turning his attention to the variety of dishes available.

Parker's eyes twinkled with mirth as he handed Melody a plate, their fingers brushing against each other. Sparks traveled up her arm and heated her cheeks. They made their way along the table and then rejoined the other K-9 officers. Captain McNeal had left the table. As had Kaitlin. Melody glanced around and found her friend standing near the beverage table alone. Melody excused herself and wound her way over to Kaitlin.

"Are you okay?" she asked, reaching for another glass of lemonade. The glass was cold in her hand.

Kaitlin gave her a small smile. "Yes, I'm fine. Thirsty."

"What's with you and Captain McNeal?"

Kaitlin sputtered. "What? Nothing."

"It didn't look like nothing," Melody mused.

"I don't know what you're talking about."

"Are you still working with his son?" Kaitlin had been doing some informal dog-therapy sessions with Caleb McNeal ever since the boy's mother had been killed in a car bomb.

"Yes, I am."

"And?"

"And Caleb was making some good progress until Rio was kidnapped. They were best friends."

"Rio missing must be hard on them all," Melody said.

Kaitlin nodded. "It is. Patrick McNeal, Slade's father, blames himself. Caleb blames everyone. And Slade, well, he's more focused on finding Rio than he is on connecting with his son."

"I'm sure he's trying. He's a good man from what I know of him."

Kaitlin eyed her. "There were rumors he was responsible for your nephew Daniel's death."

"He wasn't." Melody sipped from her lemonade.

"I'm sorry, I shouldn't have brought that up."

She cleared her throat. "It's okay."

"I don't know if I ever told you, but I'd met your sister a few times when she worked at Arianna's Diner," Kaitlin said.

"No, you hadn't mentioned that." Sadness spread through Melody. "I miss her so much."

Kaitlin laid a comforting hand on her arm. "She seemed like a sweet woman. You two have the same eyes."

As her chest ached with grief, images of her sister rose in Melody's mind. "I heard that a lot growing up."

"Did Daniel look like his mother?"

Melody nodded. She reached for Parker's arm, her grip firm. He slid an arm around her waist. She trembled. Something had unnerved her. But he'd have to wait until they were alone to question her. They walked back to their table.

He pulled out her chair and guided her into the seat. "You're sure you're okay?"

Her intense gaze held his. He could see she wanted to say something. She glanced quickly around and then nodded. "Yes, I'm fine."

Unconvinced, he sat next to her. Conversations resumed around them. Parker tried to concentrate on what was being said, but his attention centered on the woman at his side. She was pale and silent, lost in her own thoughts.

He leaned toward her. "You're sure you're okay?"

"For now."

He tucked a dark curl behind her ear and trailed his finger down her cheek. Her skin felt petal smooth. "I wish you'd talk to me."

She touched his arm and leaned closer. "Later."

He laced his fingers through hers. "I'll hold you to that."

When it was time for him to step up on the stage to perform as part of a quartet, he wished he didn't have to leave her side.

"It's okay. Go," she said, obviously sensing his hesitation. "I can't wait to hear you sing."

He glanced around the table at his fellow K-9 officers, knowing each would protect her if needed. She'd be safe until he returned to her.

He leaned in close to whisper in her ear. "We'll leave as soon as we can. Then you'll tell me what really happened."

She turned her head. Their gazes met. Gratitude softened her gaze along with something else. Something that made his heart pound.

"Yes," she breathed out.

He touched her shoulder, the skin warm and silky, then made his way to the stage.

The deep, pleasing tone of Parker's baritone voice made Melody smile. He sang the lead melody for most of the songs while the tenors and bass backed him up. With each note she found herself falling a little more in like with him. Not love. She couldn't go there. But like. Oh, yeah. She liked him a whole lot.

She clapped loudly when the quartet finished.

When he returned to the table, his eyes glimmered. "What did you think?"

"You were wonderful," she gushed, and touched his arm. "I could listen to you sing nonstop."

The pleasure on his face sent her heart rate soaring.

He leaned closer to whisper in her ear. "I'll sing for you anytime."

"He had the same dark hair but his eyes were different," Melody replied.

"Oh, how so?"

"His eyes were an unusual silver color and shaped—" Melody's gaze was drawn to a tall, distinguished couple coming toward them. Dante Frears and his pretty wife in the flesh. His expensive tux emphasized the width of his shoulders. His salted hair was shorn close to his head. His odd silvery-blue, almond-shaped eyes zeroed in on her...

"Melody, you okay?"

Kaitlin's concerned voice barely penetrated the sudden fog enveloping Melody. For a moment, the world seemed to swim as an image of Daniel superimposed itself over Dante's approaching face.

They had the same icy almond-shaped silvery-blue eyes.

Melody's breath caught, her hand loosened on the glass she held.

Could Dante be Daniel's father?

TEN

The sound of breaking glass pierced through the din of the ballroom. Parker's gaze whipped to the source of the sound along with the attention of everyone in the room. The strains of music coming from the jazz band drifted to a silence.

Melody.

Shards of glass littered the floor at her feet.

Fear punched Parker in the gut. He scrambled from his seat and rushed to her side. With a quick once-over, he assessed her for injury. "Are you hurt? What happened?"

Her gaze lifted from the mess on the floor, flicked briefly to Dante Frears and then met Parker's. "I—the glass was slippery."

Two men in waiter's uniforms approached with a mop and cleaning supplies.

"It's okay, folks, just a little mishap," Dante said and steered his wife away.

Kaitlin touched Melody's arm. "We should move out of the way and let them clean this up."

She turned her head to face him. Their lips nearly touched. Her gaze dropped to his mouth then back to his eyes. It was too easy to lose herself in the way he looked at her as if she were the only person in the room. Swallowing hard, she fought the urge to close the distance and kiss him.

"Let's get out of here," he said, his voice low and coaxing.

She blinked. Attraction sizzled between them, threatening to consume her. "Can we go for a drive? Get some fresh air?"

And some much-needed space.

The knowing look on his face said he understood exactly what she was feeling. "Brilliant idea."

They said their goodbyes quickly and made their way to his car.

"Where to?" He started the engine.

"Just drive." She sat back, trying to regain her equilibrium. What was it about Parker that made her forget herself? She nearly laughed aloud at the absurdity of the question. The answer was obvious. Everything.

"You gonna tell me what had you so freaked earlier?" Parker asked, breaking the silence. They were passing through town now. The shops were closing up for the night. A few pedestrians strolled down the sidewalks.

Jolted out of her musings, she thought back to the moment she'd met Dante Frears's gaze. Melody certainly didn't run in his circles, so she'd never seen the man up close before. He always sent his donation checks to the youth center through the mail.

So seeing him, seeing his almond-shaped silvery-blue eyes had sparked a sense of recognition so strong she'd been unable to function for a moment.

She shifted in the seat to face Parker. "I think Dante Frears may be Daniel's father."

Surprise flashed across Parker's features. "Why do you think that?"

"They have the same eyes."

He was quiet as he turned off the main road. "How can you be sure? You haven't seen your nephew in five years."

Gazing out at the looming trees of the Lost Woods ahead of them, she said, "Daniel's eyes were a different blue than Sierra's. They were almost silver just like Frears's."

"A lot of people have light blue eyes. Even Captain McNeal has them."

She shook her head. "The captain's eyes are more robin's egg blue than silver."

"For real?" he scoffed. "How do you even notice the difference?"

She rolled her eyes. "You are *such* a guy. But

it's not only their eye color that is similar. The shape. The tilt. The *look*. Daniel's eyes are exactly like Frears's."

"It could be coincidence," he stated, bringing the car to a halt in the parking lot of the entrance to the Lost Woods. Up ahead, the trailhead marker could be seen in the beam of the Mustang's headlights.

"I don't believe in coincidence."

He cut the engine. "But eye color and shape are not enough to prove anything. Certainly not to prove Dante Frears is Daniel's father."

She leaned her head back against the headrest. "That's true. And I guess it wouldn't be a good idea to go up to him and ask if he'd had a relationship with my sister."

Parker undid his seat belt. "No, that would probably be a huge mistake. He and Slade are good friends. Offending Dante Frears could damage your career."

"I suppose you're right." Still, she couldn't shake the idea that Daniel was Dante Frears's son.

"Do you hear that?" Parker rolled down his window.

Melody tilted her head to listen, trying to discern the origins of the various noises of the woods. In the distance, she distinctly heard a dog barking. "Do you think that's Rio?"

"I don't know." He opened the driver's side

door. He reached inside his jacket and withdrew his service weapon from the shoulder holster he wore. "Let's go find out."

Melody undid her seat belt, grabbed her weapon from her purse and climbed out of the car. Following behind Parker, she picked her way through the gravel parking lot as best she could, given her high-heeled sandals. When she stepped onto the trail, her heels sank into the soft dirt. She wasn't exactly dressed for a chase through the woods.

Parker paused to wait for her. She waved him on. "Go ahead. I'm right behind you."

The barking faded. The darkness swallowed them up. Light from the moon barely penetrated the canopy of tree branches. Pungent, earthy smells teased Melody's senses. She quickly lost sight of Parker on the trail ahead. Shadows shifted and swayed all around her, disorienting her.

She proceeded a little farther down the path then halted. "Parker?"

No answer.

A rustling from her left jackknifed her heart like an injection of epinephrine. She tensed. Darting for the cover of a tree, her breathing turned shallow and loud in her ears. Her finger hovering over the trigger of her gun.

A man stepped into view and her breath caught in her throat.

* * *

All around him the black forest created a dense barrier between him and his quarry. Parker stopped to listen. Silence, except for a chirping cricket or two. He could no longer hear the dog barking. He ground his teeth in frustration.

Doubling back the way he'd come, he expected to find Melody close by. But darkness hid her. Trees loomed to his right and his left. A spear of concern skewered him. "Melody?"

She stepped out from behind a tree trunk. "Here. I wasn't sure it was you."

A shaft of moonlight streaming through the branches touched on her like a beacon. Her blue eyes and dress reflected the light, making her appear ethereal.

The anxious tension in his shoulders released but a different sort of tension filled him. Longing to take her into his arms spread through him, making his pulse pound. He strode toward her, willing his heart rate to slow and pushing the longing back to the edges where he wouldn't be tempted to give in to it.

She held her weapon at her side. "Could you tell which direction the dog went?"

"North. If I had Sherlock with me, I'd have followed." But Sherlock was kenneled at the training center so Parker could attend the party. And he couldn't forget about Melody. No way was he leaving her alone out here even if she was capable of taking care of herself.

"Do you think it was your captain's dog?"

"Could be. Like I mentioned before, a shepherd matching Rio's description has been spotted in the woods since his disappearance. And let's not forget about that informant fessing up that Rio was taken by The Boss to find something in these woods."

She nodded thoughtfully. "Daniel died in the north part of these woods. Whatever The Boss is looking for is most likely tied up with Daniel and his death."

"But that was five years ago. Rio was taken only four months ago. I don't see the connection."

"The connection is these woods. They hold secrets." Her voice trembled.

He wasn't sure if he heard distress or just the effects of the cool night air. He doubted she'd admit to any fear so he went with the latter. "You're cold."

He shrugged off his jacket and laid it over her shoulders. "Come on, let's get you back to the hotel."

When they arrived at the hotel, he parked in the hotel's underground parking garage and they took the elevator straight to the tenth floor. Officer Truman was already there waiting for Melody.

"I'll say good-night," Parker said at the door.

She slipped off his jacket and handed it to him. A soft smile played at the corners of her mouth. "Thank you."

Feeling her smile all the way to his toes, he folded the jacket over his arm to keep from reaching for her. *Get back on track, Adams.* "Tomorrow I plan to take Sherlock back to the woods and see if he can pick up Rio's scent."

She glanced back through the open suite door to where Officer Truman sat in a chair reading a magazine, then gazed back at Parker. "That's a good idea. It's too bad we didn't have him with us tonight."

He smiled as her words echoed the thought he'd had earlier. They were so in sync with each other. It was a bit disconcerting and yet… he found he liked it. He wished they could be alone for a few more minutes. "Yes. Though we are hardly dressed for traipsing in the woods tonight."

Her eyes sparkled. "Too true. You look handsome in your tux, by the way."

He sucked in a quick breath at the compliment. Though he'd already told her she looked stunning, he felt compelled to tell her again, just in case she forgot. "You are beautiful."

In the dim light of the hall, he could see her cheeks flushing. Their gazes locked, held. His nerve endings came alive with the velocity of an electric current. The impulse to kiss her over-whelmed him.

With a control he hadn't had to employ in a long time, he forced himself to remain still. Kiss-ing her would be a bad idea. He'd been asked to keep her safe. And she was. The hotel was secure. She had a female officer in residence. There was no reason for him not to back away and say good-night.

Yet he didn't want to leave her. But staying was out of the question. Seeing her tomorrow was a given. "Would you want to come with Sherlock and me to search the woods in the morning?"

She blinked, a slow sweep of long lashes. "Yes. Yes, I would."

Her voice sounded a bit breathless as if she, too, were struggling with the attraction arcing between them.

He was relieved to know he wasn't the only one feeling the magnetic draw. All the more rea-son for him to be professional and rein in his longings. Tomorrow in the light of day, he'd have better control of himself. "Okay. I'll swing by tomorrow around eight."

"I'll be ready."

After a heartbeat, he turned to go.

"Parker?"

He braced himself and turned to face her. If

he didn't retreat soon, his control would slip and he'd kiss her for sure. He wondered what she'd do if he did. The question had him stepping toward her.

"I know I'm right about Dante Frears being Daniel's father."

He silently groaned. A reality check if ever there was one. He'd hoped she'd let that theory go. He understood how important figuring out what happened to her nephew was, but he was worried about her. "Melody—"

She held up a hand. "I know. The only way to prove it would be DNA. And getting Dante Frears's DNA would be difficult unless he freely gave it."

"Approaching him about it would cause problems for you and the department." Needing to touch her, to show that he cared for her, he tucked a curl behind her ear. "Don't torture yourself with this. Daniel is gone. Whoever his father was doesn't matter anymore. He can't be doing anything for the boy."

A flash of pain crossed her face.

An answering ache throbbed through Parker. "I'm sorry. I don't want to hurt you, but it's not healthy for you to continue down this path. Your memory of your nephew's eyes isn't grounds to start an investigation into one of the town's most prominent citizens."

Her mouth twisted, and disappointment lingered in her gaze. "I suppose you're right."

Although she'd acquiesced, unease slithered down his spine. He knew her too well to believe she'd drop the subject so easily. "I know you want to find answers. I want to help you. We'll keep digging, I promise. We'll find out who killed your nephew and why."

"You're a good man, Parker." She leaned in to kiss his cheek.

Her words wrapped around his heart. Tender affection bloomed as her soft lips branded his cheek. He had to dig deep down for another ounce of control to not reach for her, to pull her closer and brand her as thoroughly. He couldn't forget they had an audience. But Officer Truman wasn't as big a concern as Parker's pounding heart.

He was in trouble. Big, big trouble. And he hadn't a clue how to get out of it.

Or if he even wanted to...

"Well, that was unproductive," Melody groused.

She was tired and her feet hurt. But at least today she was prepared for a romp through the forest. Last night she'd been dressed in heels and a form-fitting dress that had not only restricted her movements but had made her feel as pretty as Parker had said.

She still had to pinch herself every time she replayed his words in her head.

Which happened several times throughout the night and this morning while they'd searched the woods with Sherlock for two solid hours hoping to find Rio's scent. The beagle had tracked a rabbit to its burrow, found a baby bird that had fallen from its nest and led them on a merry chase through the trees only to halt at a fire access road.

"Not necessarily," Parker countered. "I'm betting that access road has more traffic on it than it should. I sent the CSU team to take imprints of the tire tracks we saw. They'll compare them to the forest-service vehicles."

He held the door to the youth center open for her. She walked past Sherlock, the cord of his leash rubbing against her pant leg.

"And if they don't match, we'll know for certain someone has been using that road unauthorized." That was sound logic. And hopefully, from the impressions, they'd discover what type of vehicle had been there recently. At least it would give them something to go on. Melody hoped Rio was still alive and well. She sent up a silent prayer for Rio's safe return. So many people were waiting for the dog to come home. Most important, Captain McNeal's son.

"I'll be back at five to escort you to the hotel," Parker said after she'd unlocked her office door and pushed it open. "How about we grab dinner together?"

An excited flutter hit her tummy. Another social outing? As a protective measure…or because he had feelings for her? Did she for him? Yes. Yes, she did. Friendship, caring, affection. Nothing too scary. Nothing she couldn't handle. Or voice out loud. "Okay. Sounds good."

With a salute, he and Sherlock left. Melody entered her office and sat at her desk. There was plenty to keep her busy for the next several hours, and the time flew.

A knock drew her attention. Ally stood at the threshold of the office.

"So everything is all set for tonight's movie night."

Melody waved her in. "Good," she said. "You did a great job with the last one. I'm sure this one will be a success, as well."

Ally smiled. "I don't think I've told you how much I appreciate you giving me the opportunity to help here. Being a part of the youth center has changed my life."

Melody remembered the angry and defensive girl she'd once been. "You're welcome."

"I'm sorry I didn't tell you about Daniel before."

A shaft of grief speared Melody. "I understand. Is there anything else you want to tell me now?"

The young woman shook her head. She walked to the framed photo sitting on top of the filing cabinet, and picked up the picture of Daniel and Sierra taken a year before they died.

"I miss him," Ally whispered.

Melody's heart squeezed tight. "Me, too." And Sierra. "Can you hand me that photo?"

Ally brought it to the desk. Melody stared at the picture of Daniel, studied his eyes. The photo was taken outside of Sierra's apartment building. Sunlight reflected in Daniel's silvery-blue eyes. Eyes eerily similar to Dante Frears's.

"I want you to look at something for me." Melody turned to her computer. Her fingers hit the keyboard and a few seconds later Dante Frears's image appeared on the screen. Almond-shaped silvery-blue eyes stared at the camera in a publicity head shot.

Melody held the photo of Daniel next to the computer. "What do you think?"

Confusion wrinkled Ally's brow. "About what?"

Melody didn't want to lead her to seeing the similarity. "Look at their faces. Tell me what you see."

Ally considered for a moment. Her eyes widened a fraction. "Their eyes. They have the same eyes. Who is that man?"

"Dante Frears."

Ally's mouth formed a stunned "oh."

ELEVEN

Elated that someone else saw the uncanny resemblance, Melody was more determined than ever to find out the truth.

Jim Wheaton stepped into the office. "What about Dante Frears?"

Melody motioned him over. If he saw it, too, then Parker would have to believe her and help her figure out how to confirm her suspicion. "Dante Frears might be Daniel's father."

Jim's steps faltered then he rushed the last few feet to her side. "You're joking. Dante Frears can't possibly be your nephew's father. That's ridiculous."

"Look closer. They have the same eyes," she insisted.

Jim's gaze bounced between the two images. "No. I don't see it."

"I do," Ally stated. "And that would make sense."

"How?" Jim barked. "How could Dante Frears,

a well-respected and wealthy citizen of Sage-brush being the father of some drug-addicted punk make sense?"

Melody's temper flared. "Daniel wasn't a punk. He was a troubled kid. And my nephew."

"A kid dealing drugs," Jim shot back.

She narrowed her gaze on him. "That's only speculation." At least it had only been speculation until Ally had confessed to her yesterday that Daniel *had* been dealing. But Melody hadn't shared that information with Jim. And frankly didn't feel the need. Not with his surly attitude.

"Everyone knew it. You're the only one who wouldn't believe it," he countered.

Was that true? She searched her heart. Deep inside she knew what he said was true. She hadn't wanted to believe her nephew was deal-ing. "He had a partner."

Jim drew back. "He did? Who?"

Melody shook her head. "I don't know yet. But I intend to find out."

"You're like a dog with a bone. Let your nephew rest in peace. Stop trying to stir up trou-ble. Especially with Dante Frears. He's one of the center's top donors."

Beads of sweat rolled down Jim's temple. Overly hot or nervous? Why was everyone so afraid to upset Dante Frears? First Parker, now Jim. Just because the man had wealth enough to spare didn't mean everyone should walk on eggshells around him.

"I know that," Melody stated. "Which is why I won't say or do anything until I have proof."

"There's no proof to find." Jim's gaze narrowed. "You told me your sister wouldn't tell you who fathered Daniel. She obviously didn't want anyone to know. You should respect that and drop this whole thing."

"Daniel found out who his father was before he died," Melody informed him.

Jim pulled a face. "No way."

"I'm pretty sure he talked to the man," Ally interjected. "Daniel kept saying the guy would pay for not acknowledging him."

Jim whipped around to stare at Ally. "Did he say who this man was?"

She shook her head. "Only that the man lives here in Sagebrush."

Maybe he didn't want to acknowledge the similarities between Daniel and Dante but he saw it, Melody was sure. "Don't worry, Jim, I'm not going to do anything to jeopardize our funding."

He nodded stiffly. "I hope not. It's hard enough keeping the doors on the place open with all the rumors of drug trafficking."

Melody frowned. "We've put those rumors to rest."

He shrugged. "People have long memories."

Parker and Sherlock appeared in the doorway of the office. "Is this a private party or can we join in?"

Melody's heart did a little flip at the sight of him. He looked so good in his uniform. Though he'd been spectacular in his tux, as well. "Come in. We were discussing the rumors that the center is being used for drug trafficking."

"Sherlock and I haven't found any more, not even traces."

Satisfaction arched through Melody. "See, nothing to worry about."

Jim's mouth pressed into a thin line. "Just don't go starting any other rumors." With that he stalked out of the office, brushing past Parker and Sherlock without acknowledging them.

Parker shook his head. "Is he always so grouchy?"

"Yes!" Ally nodded in an exaggerated way.

Feeling the need to defend her partner, Melody said, "He's not a bad person. I don't think he ever really got over the death of his wife. And the center has become his whole world. He's protective of it."

"What rumors are you going to start?" Parker asked, alluding to Jim's parting shot.

She turned her computer monitor toward him and held up Daniel's photo so the two images were side by side. "You tell me."

Parker studied the images. His gaze then zeroed on her. "You're not going to give this a rest, are you?"

She shook her head.

He glanced back at the photos. "There are similarities but…"

"But you still don't think it's enough to require checking Dante's DNA?"

"We don't have the authority to do that. Even if he is Daniel's father, that isn't a police matter. Besides, what point would there be to bringing it to light now? It would only embarrass Dante."

"But it could shed some light on why Daniel was so out of control that night." She couldn't keep the pleading tone out of her voice.

"You're tenacious, I'll give you that."

Hadn't Jim said that, as well? "It's what makes me a good cold-case detective."

"True." He let out a resigned breath. "I'll talk to McNeal. But don't get your hopes up."

Pleased, she beamed. Not only were some of her questions on the brink of being answered, but also Parker believed in her enough to put himself out there by taking her suspicions to his boss. Affection flooded her heart. She could easily find herself falling for the handsome detective if she weren't careful. But letting her guard down wasn't something she wanted to do again. No matter how much she cared about Parker Adams.

* * *

At dinner last night, Melody had agreed to accompany Parker to church again. So this morning Parker headed downtown to the Sagebrush Hotel to pick her up. As he drove, he realized how happy it made him that she'd let her faith show.

Her story about her grandfather had touched him, and he was thankful she'd had such a strong and positive influence in her life. Especially given that her father and her husband had both abandoned her.

He couldn't imagine what her ex-husband had been thinking. Melody was such a tremendous lady. Kind, smart, fun. Tough, yet vulnerable. Parker had to admit, to himself at least, that she was working her way into his heart. But caring for her was as far as he could allow himself to go. Anything more would only be a disaster. He'd end up disappointing her or hurting her. Neither of which he was willing to do.

He parked in the garage of the hotel. His phone rang before he climbed out of the car. An unfamiliar number displayed on the screen. "Parker Adams."

"There's been a hit put out on a cop."

The words sent a chill down Parker's spine. He knew that voice and trusted the caller. "Harry, you better have details."

His confidential informant cleared his throat. "I'm not 411, you know. I just pass on what I got."

"Who's the hit on?"

"A detective named Zachary."

Air swooshed from Parker's lungs. Melody. He couldn't let anything happen to her. "Who put out the hit?"

"Hey, man, if I tell you that I'm as good as dead. You do your thing and protect the cop and it'll be good."

Rage built in Parker's chest. No one was going to harm Melody. "I need to know who ordered the hit."

A moment of silence met his demand. "Get me a ticket out of this town and I'll tell you."

"Done."

"Meet me at the bus station in an hour."

Parker checked his watch. "An hour." He hung up and dialed Melody's suite, his fingers clumsy on the phone.

"Hello?"

Hearing her voice did funny things to his insides. Things he chose at the moment to put on the back burner. Her safety was the priority. And he'd do anything in his power to protect her. "It's me. Are you okay?"

"Yes, fine. Are you here? I'll be right down."

The happiness in her voice tugged at him in

a way nothing else could. "No. Stay in the suite and away from the windows."

"Why?" Her voice sharpened. "What's happened?"

He swallowed past a lump of dread to say, "Someone's put a hit out on you."

Her soft gasp echoed in his head.

"I'm on my way to meet with an informant. I'll get the details. Until I return, stay safe. Fill Officer Truman in."

There was a slight pause before she said, "I will. You be careful, too."

"Count on it." He had to come back to protect her.

But first he needed to find out who wanted her dead.

The bus station at the edge of Sagebrush's main drag was busier than Parker would have guessed on a Sunday morning. People must want to start their journeys early. He spotted Harry huddled near the ticket booth. Parker casually made his way through the milling passengers waiting for the bus to open its door.

The attendant smiled a greeting when he stepped up to the ticket window.

"Where's that bus going?" Parker asked.

"Los Angeles," the attendant replied.

Parker glanced at Harry and received a subtle

thumbs-up from the older man. Parker bought a one-way ticket, then walked into the restroom. He made a quick sweep, making sure there was no one inside. A moment later Harry shuffled in.

"It's clear," Parker assured him. "Who put the hit on Detective Zachary? Was it The Boss?"

Harry shook his head. "Naw. But he works for The Boss, so it's almost the same thing."

"A name," Parker ground out.

Harry held out his hand. "My ticket."

"Not until you give me what I want."

"Another cop. Jim Wheaton."

The name punched Parker under the ribs like an upper cut. "Are you sure?"

"Yeah. I'm sure. That cop has rousted me a couple times from sleeping in the youth center parking lot. So yeah, I recognized him when he came into the neighborhood last night."

"Did you hear him say the words? Actually say he wanted Detective Zachary dead?" Parker couldn't accuse Jim of hiring an assassin to take out Melody without being absolutely sure.

"With my own ears. I saw him down on Lost Woods Road. I knew he was up to no good. I followed him. Saw him meet with a couple of thugs. Real nasty dudes. Heard him say he wanted Detective Zachary off the streets by tomorrow. He paid them a bundle of cash. Told them they'd get more when the deed was done."

Parker's fist clenched around the ticket, crumpling the paper.

"Hey, don't ruin it. You'll have to buy another," Harry snapped.

Parker handed over the ticket. "Thank you, Harry. Take care of yourself."

Harry snatched the ticket. "I always do. See you later. Or not."

He shuffled out of the restroom. Parker gripped the sides of the sink. Fury like he'd never experienced detonated in his chest. Jim Wheaton. Melody's partner and friend had put a hit out on her. She would be crushed when Parker told her. His gut clenched.

Not a task he was looking forward to, no matter how necessary. He hated the thought of causing her more anguish, but it couldn't be helped. She had to know the truth. As did their bosses. But he owed it to Melody to tell her first.

He hightailed it back to the Sagebrush Hotel and prayed with each passing second for God to give him the words to tell the bad news.

"I don't believe you." Melody stalked away from Parker while his words echoed in her head. "There's no way Jim would do anything to harm me."

Parker spread his hands. "What can I say? I'm telling you what my informant told me."

"And you trust this informant over me?"

He frowned. "What? No! But I do trust my informant over Jim Wheaton."

"Why? Why would he want me dead?" It didn't make sense. But then nothing had made sense for a long time now. From Rio's disappearance to her nephew's grave being dug up to the drugs being found in the locker at the youth center. Not to mention the break-ins and the threatening note. What was she missing?

How was Jim involved? *If* he was involved. She thought about his nervousness yesterday. She'd thought it was due to his concern for the center. What else was going on?

"Have you reported this?" she asked.

"Not yet. I wanted you to know first. I hated the thought of you hearing this from someone else."

On some level his words pleased her, but she was so upset by his news that she couldn't take the time right now to analyze what she was feeling. "Look, I've known Jim for a long time. Worked with him closely. Can we give him the benefit of the doubt until we talk to him?"

A scowl deepened the lines between his brows. His eyes grew hard and implacable.

"Please," she implored before he could refuse her. "Let me talk to him. I'm sure there's some explanation. And if it comes to it, I'll arrest him myself." Though she couldn't fathom what that explanation could be. Her stomach roiled. For a moment she thought she might lose the breakfast she'd eaten an hour ago.

Parker's expression softened ever so slightly. "For you…we'll go to his house and talk to him. But we have to inform our captains and we're not taking any chances with your safety. I'm not going to let anything happen to you. We're taking a couple of uniforms with us and getting a search warrant, just in case."

Sudden tears pricked her eyes. She wasn't even sure why. Maybe because for the first time in a very long time, someone cared about her, really cared. "Thank you."

An hour later after arranging backup and securing the warrant they were on their way to Jim Wheaton's residence. He lived in a suburb on the east side of town in a single-level ranch on a quiet street. Parker pulled the Mustang to the curb. Sherlock had his paws up on the back of her seat. His hot breath ruffled the fine hairs at her nape, but she found she didn't mind. Having the canine with them made her feel even more protected.

A blue-and-white cruiser stopped behind them. Trepidation churned through Melody. She walked next to Parker and Sherlock to the front door, and each step felt like a nail was being driven into her chest. Parker rapped his knuckles against the white painted door. Sherlock sniffed the crack of the door.

No one answered the knock.

Melody moved to the window and peered through the open blinds. The living room looked like a tornado had touched down. Tension tightened the muscles in her shoulders. Was this chaos a sign of a struggle or was this indicative of his housekeeping skills? The mess seemed out of character with the man who kept his woodworking tools neat and orderly. "I don't see him. But the place is a wreck."

"We'll have to come back," Parker stated.

"Let's check the back," Melody said, not willing to give up so easily. The man's reputation was on the line, not to mention her life. And the odds of him waiting inside to blow her head off were how high?

Using caution, she stepped off the porch and across the brown grass toward the rear of the house.

The back patio had weathered furniture beneath a faded awning. The glass slider was locked. Melody cupped her hands to the glass and peered inside. The kitchen and dining rooms weren't any better than the living room.

Her heart hammered against her ribs.

"Parker!"

"Here," he whispered from right behind her. Sherlock nudged her foot.

"Something is wrong." Was Jim a victim of violence? Had the same person who'd ransacked Melody's office and apartment now targeted Jim?

Sherlock's sudden barking shattered the silence following Melody's announcement. The dog pawed frantically at the slider, his nails scraping on the glass, at the wooden frame.

Dismayed, she lifted her gaze to meet Parker's. She'd seen the small beagle behave like this once before. At the youth center. When he'd found the stash of drugs in the locker.

"Only one thing does this for him," Parker confirmed. "Contraband."

TWELVE

The grim tone to Parker's voice slid through Melody, and she shuddered with dread. "Oh, Jim, what have you gotten yourself into?"

And what did it have to do with her? Why did he want her dead?

Parker turned to the uniformed officer who'd followed them around the house. "We need that search warrant."

A lump of apprehension stuck in her throat. Swallowing around it, she shook her head. She didn't want to believe this was happening. How had Jim become the bad guy? Worry chomped through her. "He could be inside hurt or possibly even…" A deep grief impaled her. "Dead."

Sympathy pooled in Parker's gaze. Her chest heaved as alarm reared. She'd say this qualified for exigent circumstances, which superseded a warrant. "We need to find a way in."

"Agreed." He tugged Sherlock from the door

so he could work on the lock. "Not sure I can jimmy this open."

"How about a window?" She stepped off the patio and onto the soft dirt beneath what she assumed was a bedroom window.

She could just reach the edge of the screen. Using her fingernails, she pried the screen loose and popped it out, setting it to the side. Leveraging her hands against the glass pane, she pushed sideways and it slid soundlessly open. Triumph flared.

"Jim!"

Only silence met her call. She sent up an anxious prayer. *Please, God, don't let him be dead.*

She gripped the windowsill with both hands. "Give me a boost, please."

Parker's hand gripped her elbow and tugged at her. "I'm going in," he stated with a determined note to his voice.

"I can do it," she protested, unwilling to release her hold on the sill.

"You don't know what you'll face inside there."

"I can handle it," she said.

"This is someone you know and care about."

The truth of his words sliced into her. Horrible images came to mind. Images of Jim broken and bleeding. Whatever he'd done, she didn't want him to be hurt or worse. "I—"

"Do you really want to stand here and argue?"

Parker pressed. "We're wasting time. If Jim is inside and hurt, we need to get to him now."

The unmovable expression on his face grated across her nerves. He was right of course; they needed to get in there. She released her hold on the sill and moved back.

He placed Sherlock's leash in her hand. "Hang on to him." Her hand closed over the nylon cord in a tight hold. To the remaining officer, he said, "Keep them safe."

The young cop nodded. "Yes, sir."

Melody couldn't work up any resentment at the implication that she couldn't take care of herself and Sherlock. Her only focus was on what Parker would find when he went inside.

Parker gripped the edge of the window and he easily lifted himself up, swung a leg over and disappeared into the house.

Sherlock strained at the leash, tugging her back toward the sliding glass door.

A few seconds later, Parker unlatched the door and stepped back. "He's not here."

A mixture of relief and concern raced over her. Where was Jim?

Sherlock lunged forward, ripping his leash from Melody's hands. The dog disappeared down the hall. Parker and Melody quickly followed. They found the beagle in a home office, scratching at a closed closet door. Melody's stomach clenched. Maybe Parker spoke too soon. Would they open that door and find Jim's body?

Parker took out two sets of latex gloves from the pack at his waist. He handed a set to Melody. Grimly, she accepted them. After they'd both donned the gloves, he reached for the handle. Melody braced herself. The door swung open. Sherlock darted forward. His loud triumphant barks echoed inside Melody's head. She stared at the shelves stacked with plastic-wrapped bricks of cocaine.

"Good dog," Parker said, reeling Sherlock away from the offending substance.

Her face flooded with shock and disappointment. The implications of this find couldn't be denied. A deep, welling anger expanded through her, chasing away the horror of realizing the man she'd been working with for the past four plus years wasn't what he'd seemed. She'd been duped. Her trust once again abused.

The house hadn't been tossed like she'd first assumed, otherwise the drugs would have been found and taken. These drugs belonged to Jim. And he must have been the one to stash the baggies of the white powder they'd found in the locker at the youth center. And no doubt with the intent to sell.

Stomach roiling, Melody stumbled back.

Parker's strong arms steadied her, drawing her into his tight embrace. She turned in his arms and dropped her forehead to his chest. Tears pricked her eyes but wouldn't fall.

She remembered Jim's supposed shock at seeing the drugs in the center. His feigned suspicion of the kids and volunteers. His constant barrage of complaints. All of it was to cover his real activities. Part of her wanted to still give him the benefit of the doubt, to say there had to be a reasonable explanation. But the evidence staring at her in the face taunted that idea like a schoolyard bully.

Jim was dirty. No two ways about it.

She let out a bitter sigh of resignation. Jim was another man to let her down.

She lifted her head, her gaze meeting Parker's. The concern in his eyes drew her up short.

Show no weakness.

Stepping away from him, she regained control and ruthlessly cut off her emotions. "We have to call in CSU."

"I'll take care of it."

She spun away from him while he made the call. She studied the room they were standing in. An old, cheaply made desk butted up against one wall. A file cabinet stood in the corner, stuffed so full, the drawers didn't completely close. On one wall was a white board. Puzzled, she stared at the board trying to make sense of what was written there.

"That looks like some sort of schedule," she said, walking closer to scrutinize the times and dates. With each set of numbers was a set of letters.

Parker came to stand beside her. "It does look like some sort of timetable. And the initials? Recognize them?"

"I don't know. If I thought about it hard enough, I'm sure I could come up with several people with the same initials."

"Yeah, me, too." Parker moved to the desk. "Let's see what we have here." Systemically, he went through the contents, first the top, then the drawers.

For a moment, Melody watched him. Watched the way his powerful hands handled papers and files with gentle care, keeping his contact with each to a minimum so not to smudge any prints. She studied the lines of concentration on his face, memorized the slope of his nose, the angle of his strong jaw. She'd rather keep her focus on him than the fact she was now investigating her partner.

With a sharp shake of her head, she turned her

attention to the filing cabinet. She started at the bottom rather than the top. She knew Jim well enough to know he'd think the bottom drawer safer than the one on top. Most people would begin a search at the top and work their way down, maybe even giving up before reaching the last drawer.

Melody tugged the bottom drawer out. Papers crunched against the sides. She removed two handfuls of files from the front and set them aside. When she could slide the remaining files forward, she searched the contents, starting with the last file and working her way to the front. She had no idea what she was looking for.

When she reached the last of the second batch of files, a folder caught her attention. Her sister's name jumped out at her from the label. With her heart in her throat, she removed the folder and opened the file. An autopsy report. She frowned. Why would Jim have a copy of the ME's report from Sierra's suicide?

As she scanned the report, the reality of what she was reading crashed in on her. Bile churned in her gut, and she choked back a sob.

"Melody?"

Parker's voice sounded so far away. The file trembled in her hands. She fought to control her reaction but the shock was too great. The awful truth overwhelming. She lifted her eyes and stared into his worried brown gaze.

"My sister didn't commit suicide. She was murdered."

Parker rushed to Melody's side. She looked like she might faint. He wouldn't have blamed her. The revelation was staggering. He took the report from her shaking hand and scanned the contents. His gaze slid past the particulars straight to the important part of the matter.

Probable cause of death: asphyxiation

Though a large dose of the drug zolpidem was found in her system, along with enough alcohol that alone would have been over the legal limit, there was evidence of suffocation.

Under the heading of *Marks and Wounds* the ME had written: *Petechial hemorrhaging in both eyes. Faint bruises over the mouth and nose.*

Parker's gut flinched at the image those words provoked. Someone had held their hand over her mouth and nose, cutting off her air supply. The lethal combination of drugs and alcohol plus lack of oxygen had killed her.

Official ruling: Homicide.

There was no mistaking it. The box was checked.

The medical examiner who'd signed the report in Parker's hand was the retired ME, John Bale. Parker needed to compare this signature with the one on the report that was filed with the county to know which report had been forged. If the signatures matched, then someone had paid off the ME to falsify a new report ruling Sierra's death a suicide.

"Did Jim know your sister?" he asked, wondering what the connection was between Wheaton and Sierra.

Melody shook her head. "Not that I know of." She gave a dry, humorless laugh. "But apparently there's a lot I don't know."

He tucked the folder under one arm and wrapped the other around her waist. "Come on. We'll wait for Rose and Clay outside. We'll let them do their job."

He guided her out of the office, down the hall and out the front door.

Within a few minutes the place was crawling with uniformed law personnel. Rose and Clay climbed out of the CSU van and with curt nods headed inside. Captain Drexel arrived in a brown sedan.

Melody explained the situation. Her voice was robotic; her tone detached. She was doing a good job of hiding how horrific the situation was for her. And Parker admired her strength. He hoped she didn't let the hardness settle too deep. It was one thing to compartmentalize in order to function, and another to internalize. She'd been dealt a devastating blow by learning of her partner's betrayal. And knowing her background, Parker worried she'd let this incident heighten her distrust of relationships.

Parker's own captain arrived, as well. Parker drew Slade aside and gave him a verbal report.

Captain McNeal shook his head. Sadness filtered the blue of his eyes. "Hard to believe Jim Wheaton was a dirty cop."

Glancing over at Melody, Parker's heart twisted in his chest. "Yes. But we knew there was someone within the department who was working for The Boss. At least now we can plug the leak."

"We have to find Wheaton," Slade said, his voice fierce, his expression determined. "Get him to flip. I want this supposed boss."

As did Parker. "I'd like permission to follow up on the medical examiner."

Slade nodded. "Whatever you need to do."

They turned as Captain Drexel and Melody approached. Resolve set her features into grim lines. Her bright blue eyes were hard like gemstones set against her pale complexion. Parker resisted the urge to take her hand, to offer support. Better to keep up a professional front while their bosses were present. Better to keep a distance for his sake, as well.

"Detective Zachary tells me there's a hit put out on her by Wheaton," Drexel said.

"Yes, sir. I had credible intel which led us here," Parker confirmed.

"Glad you followed the lead." Drexel leveled him with a pointed look. "Next time I'd like to know if one of my officers is in danger."

Feeling the reprimand deserved, Parker nodded. "I take full responsibility for not reporting in right away."

"Hardly," Melody interjected as her gaze locked with Parker's. "It was my idea to come here first. My wish was to give Jim the benefit of the doubt. I owed him that." She met her captain's stare. "My fault. If there's to be any consequences, I should pay them."

She was trying to protect him. Deeply moved, Parker stepped closer to her.

"I think you both were blessed this time not to have this situation turn deadly. Next time it might not go as well. Keep that in mind," Drexel said.

"Yes, Captain," Melody replied.

"Yes, sir," Parker concurred.

"Parker has asked to follow up on the medical examiner," Slade informed Drexel.

"So has Detective Zachary," Drexel commented. "They can work that angle together."

Slade inclined his head in approval.

Glad that they would be allowed to continue working the case, and together no less, Parker glanced at Melody to see how she'd take the news. Her expression was shuttered, closing off her thoughts. And it hurt way more than it should to be shut out.

Yes, he was definitely wading in too far with Melody. If he weren't cautious, he would find himself in the deep end without a life preserver. Good thing he could swim. But he had a feeling he'd drown beneath the weight of his feelings for Melody. Best to start paddling now and keep a professional and emotional distance between them as best he could.

With their mandate in place, the two captains left the scene. Parker waited a moment for Melody to say something. She seemed lost in her thoughts, her gaze on the house. Likely trying to digest all that had happened. Her partner was dealing drugs and she'd found out her sister had been murdered. He curled his fingers to keep from reaching for her hand.

"Let's head to the county coroner's office," she finally said, breaking the silence.

Glad to see her ready to work, he nodded. The central clearinghouse for the county medical reports was housed in the Sagebrush coroner's office on the other side of town. When they arrived, they signed in at the front desk and then made their way to the records room in the basement. The place was warm from the day's heat and smelled musty. Parker explained their request to the attendant, an older man with a wide girth and a lined face that seemed to hold a perpetual frown.

"Sorry, all requests must be made in writing and go through the brass upstairs," the older man stated flatly, not deigning to rise from his chair.

More like the guy didn't want to be bothered. "We don't have time for reports. This is urgent."

The man shrugged. "Them the rules."

"I'm sure Mayor Hobbs would not agree," Melody said, her voice cold. "Let's call him and find out."

Frowning, the man held up his hand. "Hold on there, missy. I don't think we need to get the mayor involved." He hefted his considerable bulk up from the chair and lumbered over to a desk with a computer. "What file do you need?"

Parker repeated what they'd already told him.

"Five years ago?" He shook his head. "Hmm, that'd be before the city installed the new-fangled computers." He pointed toward the rows of boxes behind him. "You'll have to find the file manually since we've only scanned in reports for the last three years."

Without a word, Melody marched past the attendant and started searching for the box with the right date. Parker joined her. Patience, he realized, was one of Melody's many virtues; he, on the other hand, grew antsy as time ticked by. Three hours later they located a box with the correct year written on the outside in big bold letters.

Parker took the box from the shelf and set it on the floor. Melody immediately rifled through the many files inside.

"Here we go," she said, taking a file from the box.

"Let's take it to the station," he said. "We'll have Clay compare the signatures."

Taking their find with them, they hurried down the block to the Sagebrush Police Station. The one-story brick building was thankfully air-conditioned. They found Clay in the crime lab. He was bent over a microscope when they walked in.

"Hey, Clay, we have a favor we need from you," Parker said, halting beside the quiet man.

The CSU technician lifted his head and eyed them warily. "I'm pretty busy."

"This shouldn't take long." At least Parker hoped not. "We need you to analyze two signatures and tell us if they are the same signer."

"Do you have the originals of each document? Because photocopies won't hold up in court, cuz there's too much room for error in ink placement, light fractures—"

"We have them both," Melody interjected.

"Okay, good." Clay led them to a light board. "Place both copies here."

Parker opened the large manila envelope and slid the contents out. He placed the two versions of Sierra's coroner's report on the board.

Using a handheld magnifying glass, Clay studied the signatures at the bottom of the two reports.

"These are the same," he declared.

Anger tensed the muscles in Parker's shoulders.

Melody pressed closer. "Are you sure?"

"The *J* in the name John loops slightly at the bottom of the downward stroke. They're identical. And in the last name you can see how the signer double backs over the letter A before moving on to the *L*."

Melody stepped back. "Thank you, Clay. You're a gem."

The man moved away from the light board with a shy smile. Parker took the two reports and replaced them in the manila envelope.

Stalking out of the lab, Melody said, "We have to find John Bale."

"Back to the coroner's office. They should have an address for Bale."

This time they talked directly to the current

medical examiner, Nolan Rader. The thirty-something coroner had the information they sought.

"It's so odd that you'd be asking about Dr. Bale," Nolan said as he handed over the address for the retired ME.

"How so?" Parker asked, glancing at the sheet of paper where Nolan had written out the address. Bale had retired to Corpus Christi. An hour's drive.

"Dr. Bale called last month. I hadn't heard from him since the day he left, then out of the blue…"

"What did he want?" Melody asked.

"He'd heard about the desecration of a grave. I guess it made headlines all over the state. Anyway, he wanted to know the identity of the person in the grave."

Parker and Melody exchanged a charged look. That *would* be odd if they hadn't already discovered the man had falsified Sierra Jones's autopsy report. Clearly, Melody's cold-case instincts were on high alert also.

"And you told him the person's identity?" Melody asked.

Nolan shrugged. "I didn't see any reason not to. He was the coroner of record for the boy's death."

Anger darkened her eyes. "He was probably relieved to know it wasn't Sierra's grave."

Confusion crossed Nolan's face. "Come again?"

Shooting her a warning glance, Parker cupped Melody's elbow and steered her toward the door. He didn't want to divulge what they knew. He wasn't sure who to trust. "Thank you, Doctor. You've been most helpful," he called over his shoulder.

When they were back in the station house, Parker handed Melody the address for John Bale. "You up for a road trip?"

Purpose lit her expression. "Let's do it. Let's nail this creep to the wall and find out who killed my sister."

THIRTEEN

John Bale lived in a retirement community in a posh neighborhood near Corpus Christi Bay. A place that looked too costly even for a retired medical examiner. It was more in the realm of celebrities and former big-time business moguls. But then again, Melody thought bitterly, he'd most likely been paid handsomely for his duplicity. Enough to keep him in style through his golden years. Well, she wondered how he'd like prison life.

She marched up the walkway toward the front door with Parker and Sherlock at her side. Parker wore his Sagebrush uniform, making him appear intimidating and more handsome than a man had a right to be. Even Sherlock looked smart in his chest vest with the SPD emblem. They worked well together. Both professionally and personally. A team. On so many levels.

They entered the three-story facility, leaving the May heat behind. The almost frigid air-conditioned temperature made goose bumps break out on Melody's arms.

She felt like she'd walked into a library rather than a senior citizens' center. The bottom floor opened to a central space with balconies overlooking the ground floor, making the center more cavernous than the outside suggested. The entryway was lined with bookcases filled with all sorts of books, some old and leather bound and some paperbacks. Inviting cushy chairs were placed in several small groupings allowing for intimate conversations.

An oak desk sat in the middle, manned by a pretty woman in her forties. And behind her was a game room, complete with a Ping-Pong table, a television with an electronic gaming system being used by two white-haired gentlemen. Chess tables were set up near the windows, as well.

To the right, Melody could see a dining hall with red linen tablecloths covering various-size tables for groups of two to six. It was all very appealing in a way that she found disconcerting.

When the time came would she opt for a community like this where she'd be with others her own age? Or would she grow old alone and lonely?

The question left her feeling a bit melancholy. And realization had her heart thumping. She'd always figured she'd be on her own like she'd been most of her life. But a solitary future didn't appeal the way it once had. She should make more of an effort to form connections. Healthy connections.

She slid a glance Parker's way.

One thing the last few days had made clear to her was she'd isolated herself too much.

The receptionist's eyes widened when they walked up. "Can I help you?"

Melody glanced at Parker. He gave a slight nod, letting her take the lead. She liked that because it made her feel respected. She would thank him later. He, at least, was dependable. Unlike the other men in her life.

But for how long? a cynical voice in her head asked.

She shut down the thought and focused on what she needed to do.

"I'm Detective Zachary and this is Detective Adams." Melody held out her badge for the woman's inspection. "We'd like to see one of your residents. John Bale?"

"Doctor Bale, you mean?" the woman said, her gaze raking over them warily. "You'll need to sign in." She gestured to a white binder on the counter.

Melody printed and signed her name. Parker did likewise.

The woman picked up her phone and spoke to someone on the other line. "Doctor Bale has guests. Would you be able to take them back?"

She hung up and gave them a polite, practiced smile. "One of the nurses will be up shortly to take you to see the doctor. If you'll wait over there, please." She pointed toward a grouping of chairs near a low table filled with promotional material.

Parker picked up a brochure. "Nice place. Housekeeping and meals are included." He gave her a crooked grin. "Wouldn't mind spending my golden years in a swanky place like this."

She could see Parker adapting easily to a community setting like this. As social as he was, he wouldn't grow old alone. Someday he'd marry, have a family. Be surrounded by people who loved him. People that he loved. A stab of jealousy made her look away from him.

Their lives were so different. Their futures were worlds apart. Her throat clogged.

A moment later a male nurse wearing white scrubs approached. "Officers, I'm Terrance, Doc's nurse. This way, please."

Thankfully, she didn't have to respond.

They followed him toward a set of closed double doors. He waved a key card in front of a box on the wall and the doors opened soundlessly. This part of the facility looked more like a hospital with linoleum floors, beeping monitors and antiseptic smells.

"I thought this was an independent living retirement center," Melody said, confused by this additional wing.

"We're a full-service facility," Terrance answered. "Independent living, assisted care, memory care and hospice care. We allow our residents to transition gracefully through the latter stages of life."

Obviously, John Bale had transitioned to a different stage. She prayed he'd be coherent enough to tell them what they wanted to know.

Terrance led them to a common room. Residents sat at several lounge chairs scattered about. Some had IV drips attached to their arms. Others looked frail and weak. A few slept. A large-screen television broadcasted the afternoon news in the corner. Large picture windows provided stunning views of the Corpus Christi Bay and beyond that, the Gulf of Mexico. Her heart ached for the men and women here, cut off from the outside world by glass and pain.

Terrance stopped beside the wheelchair of a man with thin patches of silver hair. A brightly colored blanket was tucked around his legs. His gaunt cheekbones stood out in sharp angles. His eyes were closed, his body still. Sherlock ventured close to sniff his feet. Finding nothing of interest, the dog lay down, putting his head on his paw.

Melody glanced at Parker. He looked as stunned as she did. To Terrance, she said, "Is Dr. Bale ill?"

"Stage four colon cancer," Terrance replied.

Despite her anger at the man for filing a false autopsy report on her sister's death, sympathy tugged at Melody. She didn't have much experience with cancer, but she knew enough to know stage four wasn't good.

Terrance touched the older man's shoulder. "John, you have visitors."

Bale awakened and for a moment looked confused, then his dark-eyed gaze cleared as he took in Parker and Melody. "Sagebrush." He let out a raspy laugh. "I knew this day would come."

"Then you know why we're here," Parker stated drily.

Bale nodded. "Can we go outside? I'd rather not have my dirty laundry aired out for everyone to hear."

Terrance reached for the handles of the wheelchair, but Melody beat him to it. She wanted the privacy as much as Bale. Nervous anticipation of what she'd learn about her sister and nephew hummed in her veins. Her fingers gripped the handles tightly. "I'll do this."

The nurse stepped back and gestured to his right. "Through that door is a path that will take you to the gardens. Don't keep him out long. A little sun is fine, but we don't want to add heat stroke to his condition."

"We won't be long," Melody promised.

Parker held the door open while she wheeled Bale out into the sunshine. The sun's rays immediately chased away any traces of a chill from Melody. They moved along the path in silence through a green lawn, flowerbeds and benches until they'd moved far enough from the facility that there was no chance anyone would overhear them.

"I assume you're here about Sierra Jones?" Bale said, his voice flat.

Melody sucked in a bracing breath.

"Yes. We found your original report," Parker replied. "Her death was not suicide, but a murder. A murder you helped cover up."

Melody pressed the wheelchair's brakes with the toe of her boot and came to stand in front of Bale. She rocked on her heels, itching to get down to it.

Parker stepped back and a little off to the left, once again letting her take charge. When this was over she was going to owe him big-time, not only in gratitude but also in respect. Not many officers would willingly take a backseat on a case. Sherlock stretched his leash to sit at her feet.

"Sierra was my sister," she said to Bale, her voice shaking with equal parts fury and grief.

Bale shaded his eyes with his wavering hand and looked up at her. "I'm sorry for your loss."

Fisting her hands, Melody tried to stay calm. "I want to know why you did it and who you're covering for."

He considered her a moment. "I'm not proud of what I did. You have to understand, it was a difficult time for me. My wife had passed on the year before. I had just been diagnosed with cancer. I had used up all our resources on my wife." He sighed heavily. "There was nothing left for me. Even my pension wouldn't have provided enough. I wanted to spend my last few years on earth in comfort. Is that so bad?"

"Was it Jim Wheaton who paid you?" she pressed, her voice sharp. She needed to understand.

Sherlock growled. She glanced at the canine. He'd moved and was facing the parking lot.

"What is it, boy?" Parker asked quietly, bending down to pet the dog. Melody shifted her attention back to Bale.

"The sum was enough to keep me here until I pass and then some." Bale dropped his hand and looked out at the ocean in the distance.

"Why did Jim kill my sister and pay you to make it look like a suicide?"

"I—"

Sherlock erupted in frantic barks.

The sickening thud of metal penetrating flesh jarred through Melody. Bale jerked forward and tumbled out of the chair. Warm blood splattered her. Horrified, she gaped at the hole in the back of John Bale's head. The shot fatal. *"Sniper!"*

Before the word even left her mouth, Parker tackled her to the ground, his body falling hard against her, knocking the breath from her lungs. Another bullet hit close. Chunks of dirt spit at her in the face. Too close.

"Come on, we've got to get to cover," Parker yelled in her ear.

She wiggled out from under him. "There isn't any!"

The nearest tree was at least 50 feet away. They'd never make it.

Parker tugged Sherlock close then yanked on the wheelchair, maneuvering the chair to provide a meager barrier between them and the gunman.

She crouched low, her gaze searching for the threat, while her hand pulled her gun from its holster. "Do you see him?"

Holding Sherlock's leash to keep him from going after the shooter, Parker reached for his cell phone. "Shots came from the parking lot. I don't have an exact position."

Heart hammering in her chest, she lay prone,

aiming toward the parking lot between the wheels of the chair while Parker called for backup.

All she saw were cars. No, wait. There was a dark shadow on the opposite side of a Mercedes that elongated the rear tire into an abnormal shape. That had to be the shooter. She took a shot. The loud retort of her gun firing echoed across the garden and rang in her ears. Her bullet embedded itself on the side of the rear well of the Mercedes. The shadow jerked, then disappeared. The sound of a car engine turning over reached her and then tires peeled against the asphalt as the shooter got away.

Frustration ran a marathon in Melody's veins. She dropped her head to her arm. Only one person had reason to want John Bale dead so he couldn't testify against him. Jim Wheaton.

A cold wet nose nudged her. She lifted her face to find herself staring into Sherlock's big brown eyes. His tongue darted out and licked her face. Tears burned her eyes. Tentatively she petted the dog, appreciating his attempt at comfort. Over Sherlock's head, she met Parker's concerned and surprised gaze.

The welcome sound of sirens filled the air. Within minutes, Corpus Christi uniformed officers descended.

Parker helped her to her feet. "You okay?"

"No." It took every ounce of control not to sag

against him. She retreated behind a numbness that kept her protected from the pain trying to claw its way to the surface. "I want to go home."

Wrapping an arm around her, she let him lead her away from the terrible scene. She forced herself to put one foot in front of the other. She had to keep moving forward. *Show no weakness.*

Parker drove Melody to the hotel so she could shower and change her clothes. Though Melody's mind was foggy with shock and grief, she appreciated his thoughtfulness. However, no amount of hot water could wash away the horror of witnessing Bale's murder. Or the certainty that Jim was the one who'd killed the man and then tried to kill her. Had he killed her sister, too? She wouldn't know for sure until they found Jim and he answered the question.

Once dressed, she sat on the small sofa in the corner of the room. She needed time to gain some control of her emotions so she could function. Despite her efforts, grief filled her to bursting. Tears welled. Her chest ached. A sob built from deep within.

She'd loved Sierra. And Daniel.

Five years ago she hadn't cried. She'd buried her grief beneath the anger and let the rage fuel her forward, determined to find justice for her nephew. And redemption for herself for not being there for Sierra. But now…the hollow places inside of Melody opened wide, threatening to swallow her up until she was nothing more than an empty shell. She buried her face into her hands, hating this show of weakness, yet unable to do anything to stem the tide of anguish overtaking her.

The sound of a knock on the bedroom door barely penetrated through her despair. The door opened. She stiffened. Desperately, she tried to stifle her crying. She wiped at the tears cascading down her cheeks. Fought to catch her breath. She kept her gaze fastened on the floor. She didn't need to look up to know it was Parker. She felt his presence like a burst of sunlight on a cold winter's day. His energy enveloped the room, making her want to partake of his heat and strength even as she despised herself for the longing. The sofa cushion dipped as he sat next to her. Without a word, his arms came around her.

A noise of distress escaped. She wasn't sure if in protest or submission. Another sob swelled. She wrestled to keep it trapped within but when he tugged her closer so that her back rested against his broad chest, she lost the battle. The sob exploded out on a gushing wave.

Slowly, he turned her to face him. Her arms slid around him, holding him tight like an anchor in a storm-tossed sea. She buried her face within the warm crook of his neck, giving herself a moment to accept the comfort he was offering.

His hand soothed over her back. His gently murmured words of comfort calmed her tears. His scent, spicy and masculine, filled her head. Awareness shimmied past the misery. She lifted her head, needing something more from him, needing to feel alive and whole. Needing to know she wasn't alone.

Her mouth found his. She felt his surprise in the tenseness of his lips, then they softened, and he kissed her back. Delving into the kiss, she lost herself in the sensations rocketing through her system, leaving a fiery trail of longing to burn her mind, her heart, her soul.

She tore her mouth from his. He dropped his forehead to hers. His chest heaved on an intake of breath, but he stayed silent for a moment.

Questions spun in her head like a whirlwind. What was she doing kissing Parker like there was no tomorrow? Kissing him as if her very life depended on it? Kissing him as if she had any right?

Where would this lead?

Nowhere.

They were colleagues. Friends, even. And no matter how much she wanted to risk trusting him with her heart, she couldn't. She wasn't that strong. She'd been down that road and found nothing but a dead end.

"I'm sorry," he finally said.

That was so like him to take responsibility that wasn't his to take. She laid a hand on his chest and eased back to look into his handsome face. "I kissed you. If anyone should apologize, it's me."

He grinned, knocking the air back into her lungs. "Okay. I take it back. I'm not sorry."

The look in his eyes sent her pulse jumping. Her lips tingled with want for more of his kisses. Obviously, the attraction wasn't one-sided but it would be foolhardy to let herself become carried away. She'd prided herself on not making imprudent choices. She thought things through, weighed the consequences, viewed her options. Kept her emotions in check.

But with him…with Parker she didn't want to be prudent. She didn't want to make the wise choice to walk away while she had the opportunity. She didn't want to withdraw her arms from around him.

No, what she wanted to do was release the impulsive side that had to be in her DNA if her sister's life was any indication.

And look where Sierra had ended up because of her impulsiveness.

The thought rocked Melody to the core, shaking up all the reasons why she'd held herself firmly apart from others. Even her ex-husband. Truth be told, she assumed some of the blame for her ex-husband's abandonment. She could have followed him, fought for the marriage. But that would have required losing too much emotional control. Control she couldn't give up now.

Slowly she extracted herself from Parker's embrace. "This can't happen."

"What can't?"

Was he deliberately being obtuse? "Us. I shouldn't have kissed you. It was a moment of insanity. I let my grief get the better of me."

He trailed a knuckle down her cheek. "Holding all that anguish in isn't healthy."

"Neither is kissing you," she retorted glumly. It didn't matter how much she enjoyed the kiss. It had been a mistake. A lapse in judgment and good sense.

"It was a kiss, Melody. You won't die from a kiss," he remarked wryly.

Maybe not physically. But emotionally? Oh, yeah. That was a slippery slope if ever there was one. And she had no intention of sliding into the abyss. She stood and glanced at the open bedroom door, using the excuse of the other woman in the living room of the hotel suite as a means to change the subject. "I'm sure Officer Truman must be wondering what's going on in here."

"I sent Patty to pick up takeout. I hope you like chow mein and chicken fried rice."

His kindness once again softened her, making her regret that this thing between them couldn't ever go anywhere. She couldn't let it. "You are a very thoughtful man."

He made a noise in his throat. "If I were that thoughtful I wouldn't have taken advantage of your misery and kissed you, especially if I'd known you'd regret it."

"I kissed you," she reminded him. "I don't regret the kiss." The admission heated her cheeks. "It's just…I'm not ready to be in a relationship. I don't know if I'll ever be."

His eyebrows plucked together. "Melody—"

The outer door to the suite opened. Officer Truman returning with their dinner. Melody wasn't sure she'd be able to eat, but she used the opportunity to escape.

What she'd said to Parker was true. She didn't know if she'd ever be ready or willing to give enough of herself, relinquish enough control, to be in a relationship again. Not even with someone as wonderful and charming as Parker Adams.

The thought left her feeling depressed.

But she had no choice. Not if she wanted to keep from being hurt again.

From this moment forward, she had to maintain a boundary to protect herself. But how, she didn't know. Especially when her heart wanted to be as close to him as possible.

FOURTEEN

With his fork, Parker pushed his noodles around on his plate. His appetite was nonexistent. He forced himself to eat to keep up his strength, because the last thing he needed was to be groggy from lack of food. Not with so much at stake. But he was having a hard enough time getting his brain to function with memories of Melody's kiss burning a hole through his head.

Saying he'd been surprised when she pressed her soft lips to his would be an understatement. She'd tasted like salty tears and sweetness. For a fraction of a second he'd thought to resist, but then his whole body responded. Kissing her back had sent his senses careening out of control like a racecar taking a turn without a skid block to keep the bottom from hitting the track.

A major violation if ever there was one.

He'd vowed to keep her safe. He hadn't realized he'd be the one needing protection from her. But when he'd heard her crying, he'd been unable to keep himself from going to her. He'd felt so powerless in the face of her anguish…and couldn't help but reach for her. Holding her had been the only thing he could think to do.

Kissing her had been pure pleasure. And pain, because the rational part of his brain told him he shouldn't. He shouldn't get involved. He shouldn't get attached. He'd only end up disappointing her in the end, just like he had his family. His brother's death was an emblem he wore as a reminder of his failure. He hadn't been there for him when he should have. The only way to make sure he never let anyone else down was to not get involved. Not get too close.

I don't regret the kiss. The statement pleased him more than he thought possible, more than was wise. He was hard-pressed to say given the same chance he'd do anything differently.

I'm not ready to be in a relationship. I don't know if I'll ever be.

This, he understood. Because he was right there with her. Her reasons were clear to him. She'd been hurt badly by her father, then her husband. Now Jim. Men who should have stuck by her through all of life's ups and downs. But they hadn't. They'd left her. Betrayed her. Making her feel somehow there was something wrong with her. He'd told her there wasn't. And he wished he could find a way to prove it to her once and for all. But he couldn't. Doing so would only set her—and himself up for more heartache.

Lord, what do I do here? How do I protect us both. Parker's cell phone rang. He answered. Shock siphoned the air from his lungs, and it took a moment for him to find his voice. "We're on our way."

He clicked the phone off and met Melody's anxious gaze. A knot of dread formed in his gut. Though it would cause her more pain, he had to tell her. He took her hand.

She gripped his arm, obviously sensing something was wrong. "What's happened?"

"The Sagebrush Police have Jim trapped in a stand-off."

Alarm filled her eyes. "What? Where?"

"The youth center."

"He's still holed up in the woodworking room," Captain McNeal informed them when they arrived at the makeshift command post— the back of a tactical van parked down the street from the center.

The only light showing in the brick building came from the room where Melody knew Jim spent most of his time. From the moment Parker had informed her, she'd felt like she was in a daze. Jim was in a standoff at the youth center. The youth center they'd built together. They'd done so much good there, helped so many kids and had made a difference in not only the teens' lives but the whole community's. And now he was destroying that. She tried not to tremble with the shock.

FBI Agent Trevor Lewis joined them. "We've tried negotiating. He's not cooperating. The state police are assembling and plan to breach the building in ten."

"Are there hostages?" Parker asked.

Panic trapped the air in Melody's lungs. Her gaze searched the darkness and picked out the men dressed in tactical gear, ready to initiate a full-on assault of the center. Her throat closed with alarm. Penetrating the center would be a last-resort move. She prayed it wouldn't come to that.

"Yes. There's at least one," came Slade's grim reply.

"Who?" Melody asked, and winced at the slight quiver in her voice.

"Ally Jensen."

Anguish stabbed her. *Oh, no. Poor Ally.*

She had to do something. The youth center was her responsibility. Determination burned through Melody. She had to reach Jim, make him see how futile his actions were. There was no way this could end well if he didn't cooperate.

She squared her shoulders and lifted her chin. "Let me talk to him."

"Absolutely not!" Parker exclaimed.

Irritation set her teeth on edge. "It isn't your call."

Captain McNeal's eyebrows rose nearly to his hairline. Melody wasn't sure if it was in response to her request or to Parker's vehement refusal. She jerked her gaze to Parker.

Thunderclouds darkened his face. "You are too close to this. Too emotionally involved."

She couldn't deny his assertions and wouldn't even try. "I can stay in control." She turned back to Captain McNeal. "I've had hostage negotiation training through the Austin PD. I can do this."

Before McNeal could respond, Parker interjected, "It's too dangerous."

Wheeling to face Parker, she said, "You heard Special Agent Lewis. They're planning a breach in ten. Whatever Jim's done, it's not worth losing his or Ally's life over. Which could happen if this situation turns into a battle." Unconcerned by the fact they were surrounded by his captain, FBI agent Trevor Lewis and a multitude of other officers, she placed a hand over his heart. "He knows me. I'm the best shot we have."

"I don't want you to get hurt," he said, his voice dropping to a low timbre that worked its way down to her soul. "Jim wanted you dead."

For reasons she chose not to examine, she needed him on her side. "Putting ourselves in danger is part of the job."

"I don't care about the job at the moment." Worry lit his brown eyes. "It's you I'm worried about."

Any annoyance melted in the face of his concern. It was her turn to implore him to understand. "I know it's a risk. But some risks are worth taking."

He closed his hand over hers, trapping her hand firmly against his chest. "Is this one of them?"

His words reverberated through her. "I have to try." She pulled out the one card she knew would work to sway him. "If I don't attempt to talk him out, I'll regret it the rest of my life. Ally is just an innocent kid."

He closed his eyes as if pained. When he opened them, the respect there shored up her confidence and made her realize that her feelings for this man had gone way beyond anything she could control. "You promise me you'll be careful?"

"Of course."

Please, God, don't let anyone get hurt.

With her heart pounding and her breath threatening to seize, Melody stepped closer to the speakerphone. It had taken a good deal of persuasion on Parker's part to convince Captain McNeal and Agent Lewis to let Melody have a chance to coax Jim out.

Parker's belief in her touched her, yet made her wary at the same time. She was placing too much trust in this man, but that was an issue to be dealt with later. Right now she had a job to do.

Oh, Lord, give me strength and help me to know the right words to say. She sent up the silent request and inhaled deeply, calming herself. Pursing her lips, she blew out a breath and found her center. FBI Agent Lewis gave her the nod to proceed.

"Jim, this is Melody."

The silence sent a wave of uncertainty crashing through her. Would her presence make the situation worse?

"You shouldn't be here," he finally said.

Because I should be dead? The thought streaked through her mind. She bit on her lip to keep the words in. "Jim, this isn't you. You're a great guy. You love the center. You've worked so hard to make it successful."

"You don't know me," he barked. "You don't know what I've done."

She closed her eyes, mustering her strength. She thought she knew him. She'd also thought she'd known her father and her ex-husband.

"Okay, Jim. That's fair. I don't know you as well as I thought I did."

She did have an inkling of what he'd done, but saying so wouldn't be prudent. "I'd like to know you better, Jim. Let me be your friend like you've been mine."

She opened her eyes and met Parker's steady, encouraging gaze. "This is just a big misunderstanding, right, Jim? You haven't done anything that can't be undone."

"You couldn't leave it alone," he yelled. "I told you to leave it alone. This is your fault."

Drawing on the training she'd had at the Austin police department, she stayed calm, focused and refused to rise to the bait of his words. Instead, she redirected the conversation. "Jim, are you injured? Is everyone okay? Ally? I'm sure she's confused and scared. Who else is there?"

"We're fine in here as long as you all stay out there," Jim said.

"We'll stay put." She glanced at the men around her, willing them to do as Jim was asking. "No one's been hurt yet. It's not too late to make this right. You can make this right, Jim. Let Ally go. Let... I'm sorry. Who else is with you?"

Silence met her question. Each passing second tightened the knot of anxiety squeezing her chest.

"Joy," he finally answered.

An image of the teen ran through Melody's mind. Her heart ached. The fifteen-year-old must be terrified. "Joy Haversham is with you. Okay, I'm sure she and Ally would like to go home. They deserve to go home, don't they, Jim? You can make that happen for them."

"Then what? I don't have any leverage," he rasped out.

The strain in his voice worried Melody. She knew from her training that when a hostage taker felt cornered, they tended to react violently. "What can we—I—do to make this right? I want to help. Please let me help you."

"You can't. Not now."

The harsh sound of the phone slamming down echoed in Melody's head. Disappointment and anxiety spiraled through her, and she struggled to remain calm.

Parker wrapped an arm around her. "You did good."

Leaning into him, she shook her head. "He hung up. I failed."

"No, you haven't," Trevor stated, his dark eyes sincere. "We know he has two hostages. That's more than we knew ten minutes ago. We'll call him back in a few minutes."

The waiting stretched Melody's nerves until she thought she'd scream. Thoughts of what could go wrong ran through her head, making her incredibly antsy. Only Parker's comforting arm around her held her together. His calming presence was a Godsend on so many levels.

She'd be crawling out of her skin with worry if not for him. She hadn't realized how much she needed Parker's backing. Knowing he believed in her gave her the confidence to see this ordeal through. She didn't know what her life would be like when they no longer were working so closely together.

At the moment thinking about that was more than she could bear.

Four minutes later, she was given the go-ahead to try again. Her heart bumped against her ribs.

"You can do this," Parker whispered close to her ear as Agent Lewis dialed the center's landline again.

She laid a hand on Parker's arm in gratitude.

When Jim came back on the line, she said, "Jim, you said this is my fault. I take responsibility. I'll make it right. Tell me how I can make it right."

"All your questions. All your snooping. It has to stop."

Steeling herself against taking offense, she kept her voice steady. "You're right. I do ask a lot of questions. We've worked together for a long time, Jim. I didn't realize my curiosity bugged you. I can change. Come out so we can talk about that. You can help change my ways," she said, hoping the carrot would be taken.

He scoffed. "Why did you bring him in? *I'm* your partner. And that dog! I hate dogs!"

Mind reeling, she glanced at Parker. His eyes narrowed in speculation.

Jim was jealous of Parker. She wasn't sure how to respond to that.

Agent Lewis made a motion with his hand, wanting her to keep talking. "I can see how that would upset you. I had no idea it would. But now that I do, we can remedy that. Parker and Sherlock don't need to come to the center again. It can go back to being you and me. A team."

Parker tucked in his chin. She shook her head, hoping he'd realize she was trying to appease Jim. That she had no intention of barring Parker and Sherlock from the center. They'd added so much. The kids had grown used to seeing Parker and they all loved Sherlock.

"The damage is done." The resignation in his tone sent a chill of dread gliding over her skin. "I'm a dead man no matter what I do."

His words sent alarm surging through her. She had to dispel that thought. "It may seem hopeless right now, but it's not. Jim—"

The gentle click of the receiver as he hung up was worse than when he'd slammed the phone down. Panic gripped her. "Get him back."

Lewis redialed. Nothing. They tried for several minutes before Lewis shook his head. "He's left us no choice." He turned to the tactical teams leader. "You have permission to go in."

"No!" Melody's legs trembled. She nearly toppled over, but Parker held her upright.

"Can we get a chair?" he asked.

Someone brought over a small stool.

"Sit," Parker instructed.

"I can't." Sharp talons of torment clawed at her. "This is my fault. I couldn't talk him out of it."

Parker took her hands in his. "No. This isn't your fault. He brought this on himself. You did your best. All we can do now is pray for a good outcome."

She tightened her fingers around his. Grateful for his steady presence, for his faith. "Would you?"

"Of course." He drew her away from the command post to a secluded spot where they could have a moment of peace. "Lord, we ask for Your presence here. You know the situation. You know how dire it is. We ask for protection over Ally and Joy and the men going in after them…and Jim. Please bring them all out safely. Amen."

"Amen." She tugged on Parker, drawing him toward the action. "I want to get closer. I need to see what's happening."

They made their way to where Captain McNeal and Agent Lewis had taken a position with a clear view of the front of the building. A dozen or so men, dressed from head to toe in black tactical gear, prepared to enter the building. Melody's heart pounded so hard she thought she might break a rib.

The leader motioned with his hand, signaling it was time to breach the center. Melody braced herself. Just as the men stepped forward in a unified movement that spoke to the intense training and harmony of their division, the front door to the center opened. Melody's breath hitched. Was Jim giving up?

With a raised hand, the leader halted the men.

Ally and Joy came out, their hands held up in the air.

Behind them, Melody could make out Jim's balding head. She let out a small sigh of relief. He was coming out. "Thank you, God."

Then Jim shoved Ally and Joy. They stumbled forward. Two tactical team members grabbed them and pushed them out of harm's way. Jim was left exposed in the center of the doorway, a sniper rifle in his hands, the barrel pointed skyward in his outstretched hand. A dozen red dots glowed bright dead center on Jim's chest.

A small gasp escaped Melody. *No. No. No.*

She didn't want to believe this was happening. She clutched Parker's hand.

The tactical team had Jim in their sights. She was sure he'd surrender now. Prayed he'd surrender. He had to. If he didn't…she couldn't let herself go there. God would protect him just like He had Ally and Joy.

"Come on, Jim," she said beneath her breath, willing him to do the right thing, the only thing, and turn himself in.

"Drop your weapon," a harsh voice rang out, commanding Jim to relinquish his hold on the rifle.

For a breath-stealing moment, Jim didn't move. His gaze roamed the crowd of law enforcement circling the front of the building. He zeroed in on Melody.

She released Parker's hand. The sadness on Jim's face made her step toward him, wanting him to know she was here to help him. She would stand by him, help him the way she hadn't been able to help Sierra and Daniel.

Jim's gaze drifted to Parker beside her and twisted with anger and jealousy.

In one swift move, Jim raised the rifle and sighted down the barrel, his aim directed at Parker.

Chaos exploded around her. Shouts for Jim to drop his weapon rang in the night.

Parker yanked her behind him, turning so his broad back acted as a shield.

A single shot rang out.

Melody winced.

Parker's body stiffened. His arms tightened around her. For a panicked moment the horrible thought that he'd been hit stormed through her mind.

"Melody?"

Parker's voice splintered her terror. She leaned back to look into his dear face. "You're okay?"

His grim nod didn't reassure her. Something was wrong. Then her mind kicked into gear and processed what she'd heard.

One shot.

Parker hadn't taken the hit. That meant...

With a certainty she wanted to refute, she knew Jim hadn't fired his weapon. A police sharpshooter had taken the shot.

Jim was dead.

A cold numbness swept through her like an eerie fog. A weight pressed down on her chest.

Her partner.

Her friend.

She extracted herself from Parker's arms. With slow, deliberate steps she walked to where Jim's body lay on the center's steps. Blood pooled on the cement.

Tears rolled down her cheeks. Anger choked her. God hadn't answered her prayer. At least not all of it.

Her gaze sought Ally and Joy. They huddled together. A female officer comforted them. The young women were safe. And Melody was grateful for that blessing.

But Jim...

Her attention returned to the prone body of the man at her feet. The man who had wanted her dead.

One of the tactical team members had pushed Jim's rifle aside. She stared at the long, deadly weapon. Her pulse spiked. "Parker!"

"Here," he said from close behind her.

She reached for his hand and swallowed back the bile rising to burn her throat. "Is that—?"

He drew in an audible breath. "Looks like a FN SPR. 308."

Her heart thudded. "Like the one that killed Daniel?"

"Exactly like. Only ballistics can confirm it."

She staggered backward, nearly missing a step. Parker caught her. His strong, safe arms held her steady, keeping her from disintegrating into a glob of anguish and despair.

Any chance she had of learning the truth behind her nephew and sister's deaths had died with Jim. Now she would never know what had really happened. Now she would never be able to make things…right.

FIFTEEN

"Why did he do it?" Melody's tortured whisper echoed inside Parker's car.

He hated seeing her so distraught. When she'd almost fainted on the steps after realizing the rifle Jim carried matched what they believed to be the weapon that killed Daniel, he'd propelled her away from the scene. She needed to process what had happened.

Better to do it in a safe, familiar environment. It would take time to heal from this wound and the quicker she put it behind her, the better. This ordeal had taken a devastating toll.

At a stoplight, he reached to take her cold hand in his. "I'm so sorry."

"I should have seen that something was wrong." Self-recrimination echoed in her voice. "All the signs were there. His nervousness, his furtive activities." She let out a tortured laugh. "His seeming dedication to the center was all a sham. How could I have missed that?"

"You were too close to it. You trusted him. There was no reason not to. We all did." Okay, Parker hadn't fully trusted him, not after the way he'd treated Sherlock. The light turned green. He stepped on the gas but kept his hand on hers.

A half scoff, and half sob escaped her throat. She extracted her hand from his. "You'd think I'd know better than to trust. Even God let me down tonight."

Appalled that she'd think that way, he said, "No, He didn't. We prayed for protection for Ally and Joy, as well as Jim. He came through for us. Ally and Joy are safe now."

"And Jim is dead."

Parker touched her arm. "But he had a chance to save himself. He's dead by his own choice."

There was no doubt in Parker's mind Jim Wheaton had chosen to end his life on the steps of the center by forcing the tactical team's hand to avoid facing a prison sentence.

"You can't blame God for that. He gives each of us free will to choose for ourselves how we'll act, whether we'll choose good or evil."

"Right. You're right." She shifted away, out of his reach. "Jim was stuck between the police, prison and The Boss. I guess he didn't like his options."

"Did he admit to working for the crime syndicate?"

"Not in so many words." She rubbed at her

forehead. "He said he was a dead man either way. I can only assume he meant he feared The Boss would get to him."

Parker's hands flexed on the steering wheel. "He probably could have identified the crime lord."

"Yep. But we'll never know what secrets he harbored, will we?"

His gut clenched at the bitter tone to her voice. "You'll have some closure in Daniel's death if the ballistics come back a match to Jim's rifle."

"Closure? Hardly. All that report will tell me is Jim fired the shot that killed Daniel, but it won't tell me why. Or why he killed Sierra. The *why* is going to haunt me the rest of my life."

Parker wished he could refute her words, but there was too much truth there. They would never know why. But at least she was safe from Jim now.

However, a niggling feeling of disquiet tugged at Parker. "Could Jim have been the guy dressed all in black that ransacked your office?"

She shifted in the passenger seat to stare at him. "Maybe. It all happened so fast… The man seemed bigger to me, but it could have been the shock of interrupting the intruder that made him appear so large and scary."

An uneasy tension settled between them. "But

you can't be certain, which means you could still be in danger."

She shrugged and turned to face the front window. "I suppose. But once again, why?"

Frustration echoed in her words and reverberated through him. They still didn't know what the masked man had been looking for in her office and her apartment. They suspected it was the code. If only they knew what that was. Jim probably had known. Though their search of his house revealed nothing helpful on that score.

As he pulled into the hotel's parking garage, Parker's cell phone rang. The caller ID showed the police station's number.

"Adams," he answered.

"Parker, Slade here. How is she?"

Sliding a glance at Melody slumped in the seat next to him, he said, "Holding it together."

"Good. She's strong. She'll get through this."

"Yes." And Parker would be there to make sure she made it through this ordeal in one piece. She'd come to mean a great deal to him, more than he'd thought possible. No matter how much he wanted to remain emotionally detached from the pretty detective, she had worked her way beneath the protective barrier around his heart.

He loved her.

The thought rocketed through him, leaving behind a white-hot trail of shock. He leaned his head back against the headrest. He loved Melody. He wasn't sure how to deal with the realization. He certainly couldn't declare his feelings to her. Not now while she was grieving and full of anger.

"I need you and Sherlock to meet me at the Lost Woods," Slade said, drawing Parker back to the conversation.

"When?"

"As soon as you can. I want to have Sherlock try to find Rio."

"We were there this morning, Slade. Sherlock didn't pick up on his scent."

"I know, I read your report. All the sightings of Rio in the woods have been at night. I have a feeling that with Jim's death The Boss might get overconfident and show up more often. I want us to be out there waiting for him when he does."

Parker was tempted to tell Slade no. Parker didn't want to leave Melody. She was hurting and he wanted to be the one she turned to for help.

If they caught the crime lord and brought him to justice, Parker would have no legitimate reason to stick close to her. Unless…he admitted his feelings.

And risked her rejecting him because she couldn't trust anyone.

Was he ready to take that risk?

No. He needed time to absorb this shocking truth and make a plan on how to proceed.

"We'll be there in twenty," he told Slade, and hung up.

"Be where?" Melody asked, her blue eyes luminous in her lovely face.

"My captain wants Sherlock to try to track Rio again."

"Tonight?"

He nodded. "I'll walk you up. Officer Truman should be there waiting for you."

"I want to go home, back to my apartment."

He understood her need to go home, but couldn't allow it. "I'm sure you do. But you know you can't. Not yet. We don't know if you're out of danger."

"I can't live in a hotel forever," she stated, her voice flat.

"It won't be forever."

"You can't make that promise," she said. "You can't promise you'll bring down the crime syndicate or predict when. At some point, I have to return to my life. I can't keep living like this. I need to get back to normal." Her voice caught on the last word.

His heart twisted. She was grieving and not taking into account the possibilities that her life could still be in danger. "You're safer at the hotel. Jim put a hit out on you, remember?"

"But with Jim dead, there's no one to pay for the deed, right? That's no longer an issue."

"We can't be certain that's true."

Her fingers curled into fists. "I wonder what my life is worth?"

"Don't go there," he said, worried that self-pity would take a hold of her. "You're worth more than any amount of money there is."

"Careful, Parker, I might think you care," she shot back.

"I do, Melody. I love you." The words were out before he could call them back. His breath caught and held.

In the dim glow coming from the overhead parking lights, her eyes widened with what he hoped was joy, but she remained mute.

A charged silence filled the car. Parker's heart hammered so hard in his chest he was surprised the whole car wasn't rocking from the vibrations.

Melody closed her eyes. A spasm of pain crossed her face.

An unnerving dread choked Parker.

She pressed her lips together. Then she took a breath, her shoulders rising and lowering as she exhaled. When she finally opened her eyes, the total lack of emotion shining in the swirling blue depths sent his stomach plummeting.

"I'm sorry, Parker. I can't. I can't do this." She turned away from him to climb out of the car.

A deep, welling pain carved out a hole in his heart. He dropped his head to the steering wheel. It was better this way, he told himself. He'd known surrendering to his feelings would put himself at risk of disappointing her, failing to live up to her expectations. Yet, he'd hoped with Melody he could be the man she needed.

He'd known she wasn't interested in romance. Too many men had hurt her in her life to trust again.

It had been wrong to profess his love and expect her to feel the same back.

Forcing himself to move, he climbed out and escorted her to her hotel suite, careful to keep a distance. A distance he should have maintained all along.

After Parker left her hotel suite, Melody placed her holster and weapon on the dresser with care, double-checking the safety. Her insides quivered with a strange mix of regret and sorrow and possibility. Flipping off the light switch, she collapsed face-first on the bed in a weepy mess.

The darkness, broken only by the faint glow of the living-room light seeping in from beneath the bedroom door, allowed her a sense of privacy. Truman was out in the living room. But here alone, in the suite's bedroom, Melody could break down.

Her mind reeled. Pain throbbed in every fiber of her being.

I do, Melody. I love you.

Parker's words played over and over in her head like a CD stuck on a scratch.

Part of her wanted to shout with joy. Hearing those words from him was a dream come true. He made her feel special, cared for, loved. Every act, every gesture had pointed to his growing feelings. She saw that now. She should have realized long before that she'd let her guard down around him.

Who was she kidding? She'd fallen for him almost from the moment he had strode into the youth center all swagger and charm.

Yet her self-preservation was too strong. Her trust broken and abused too often to think she could really risk finding lasting happiness with Parker.

With anyone.

Parker had said God gave her free will to choose. She was choosing life without love. Life without the risk of betrayal and hurt.

That's what she wanted. What she needed. She would learn to live with this throbbing pain in her heart. It would scab over like the other wounds and she would be fine. Okay, not fine exactly, but she'd survive.

But just barely.

And really, what more could she hope for?

Spent, her tears dried and her heart aching, she flopped onto her back. Her backpack-style purse dug into her flesh. She hadn't realized she still wore the bag. She shrugged the straps off her shoulders and dropped the purse on the floor. Lying prone, she stared at the shadowed ceiling, praying for the abyss of sleep to take her away from the thoughts marching through her head.

The youth center wouldn't be the same without Jim. He'd been such a big part of its conception and implementation. A fixture.

But she had to believe the center would survive. It would take some adjustment and time. Lots and lots of time.

Just as it would take her time to figure out how to live without Parker.

Oh, they'd still see each other on occasion. But that was all she dared. Life would somehow go back to the way it was before he stormed into her world, upsetting all her carefully constructed ideas of keeping her heart safe.

But any contact would be torture. Seeing him, being near him but knowing she had to refrain from confiding in him, from depending on him. From loving him.

She wanted to do all of that and more, but she was too afraid. Too afraid to give herself over to the uncertainty, always wondering when the day would come that he, too, would leave her or betray her, when he would destroy her trust.

A thump from the outer room of the suite raised the hairs on her arm. She bolted upright.

Officer Truman had probably bumped into a table.

Still, Melody strained to listen.

The slight squeak of the bedroom doorknob turning knifed through her. She rolled off the bed and crouched on the floor, reaching for her sidearm. She grimaced with frustration. She'd left her weapon on the top of the dresser.

The door swung open. Light flooded the room. The dark silhouette of a man filled the space.

A man wearing a ski mask. His eyes blacked out. He held a gun.

Her heart hammered against her ribs. She wedged herself under the bed. On her belly, she inched herself toward the other side. If she could reach her purse, she could call for help.

A hand closed over her ankle. She kicked for all she was worth.

Please, dear God, save me.

SIXTEEN

Parker allowed Sherlock a long lead as he and Slade cut a path through the underbrush of the Lost Woods. The dog led Parker and Slade deeper into the woods, away from the trail, the earthy scents of the woods filling Parker's nostrils. He could only imagine how much more intense the smells were for Sherlock.

The bobbing glow from his flashlight bounced off tree trunks and thick tangles of leaves and branches. So far they hadn't seen any sign of Rio or the masked man. Patience, he told himself. Catching the guy might not happen tonight. But it would happen. The Boss couldn't stay hidden forever.

The woods were quiet.

Unlike Parker's thoughts.

He couldn't believe he'd blurted his feelings to Melody like that. He knew better. He had already told himself to wait because she was in shock and grieving. He didn't blame her for withdrawing and putting up a wall between them. He'd ambushed her with his declaration without a thought of the consequences.

Had his subconscious somehow known that admitting his love would send her running?

The realization slammed into him.

Had he sabotaged their relationship only subconsciously? Or was he counting on her rejection so he wouldn't have to risk disappointing her? Perhaps, deep down, he didn't trust her enough to love him despite his flaws.

Suddenly the landscape of his life spread before him, and he saw that he'd run from every relationship for this very reason. He didn't trust anyone to love him enough.

Wow, he'd thought Melody was the only one with trust issues. He sucked in a sharp breath.

"You okay?" Slade asked.

"A root in my way." A deep one.

I know it's a risk. But some risks are worth taking.

Melody's words rushed back to him. She'd been talking about the situation with Jim, but she could have easily been referring to herself and Parker. They both were so afraid to trust. How could they overcome their fears?

Certainly not by being apart.

He remembered the way his parents had fought for their marriage after his brother died. They could have easily separated, each one dealing with their grief and pain alone. But they hadn't. They'd forged ahead together, as a team, a couple. Their love was stronger for it now. Parker wanted what they had, to follow their example.

He'd have to make Melody see they were stronger together than apart. They were meant to be a team, a couple. He loved her and would have to convince her he could be trusted. And he'd do everything in his power not to disappoint her, but he would have to trust that their love would be deep enough that she would love him no matter what.

There were no guarantees in life. However, Parker had faith that God would see them through.

He pulled out his phone, intending to call her.

"Problem?" Slade asked in a low tone, reminding Parker where they were and why they were out in the woods.

Parker pocketed the phone. "No. I was just thinking about Melody."

"It was a rough night for her."

"Yes." A rough night, day, week. Actually she'd had a rough five years of grieving for her sister and nephew.

Though Parker didn't know how they'd ever discover why Jim had done what he had, he could at least help Melody discover if Dante Frears was Daniel's father or not and put that question to rest. "Slade, Melody and I have something to discuss with you."

"My door is always open," Slade replied in a low tone. "You've become close to Detective Zachary."

Parker was glad for the shadows to hide the heat creeping up his neck. "Yes. Though I blew it tonight."

"How?"

"I told her I loved her."

Slade whistled through his teeth. "That's big. I take it she wasn't thrilled to hear this."

"Not really." The image of her face when he'd told her rose in his mind. For the briefest of moments he'd seen a flash of joy. And that one moment gave him hope. Hope he would cling to. "But I'm not going to give up."

"Good. She deserves happiness. You both do."

Sherlock erupted in a frenzy of barking. Parker and Slade hurried to where the dog pawed at the ground beneath a bush at the base of a tall cottonwood.

"What is it, boy?" Parker knelt down beside the dog. The beagle dug his nails into the ground, grinding up fallen leaves and spraying dirt. His barks echoed through the trees.

Slade removed a small trowel from his utility belt and handed it to Parker. "Here."

While Slade shone the flashlight on the spot, Parker scraped away decomposing leaves and dug the sharp tip of the trowel into the dirt. He dug for several minutes before the trowel hit something hard. Sherlock howled.

"Sit," Parker commanded.

The dog obeyed with another mournful bay.

Slade slid on gloves and then dug around the embedded item. They managed to wrench the square plastic container out of the ground. Parker pried the lid open, releasing a rancid odor. His stomach heaved. His eyes watered.

Sherlock let out another long howl. The inside of the container was rimmed in a yellow film that also coated the sides of a brick of cocaine wrapped in plastic, tinfoil and duct tape. One corner of the brick had been eaten away allowing the white substance to leak out. A dead beetle lay on his back next to the hole.

Grimacing, Slade asked, "What is that smell?"

"Not sure. Something meant to disguise the scent of cocaine. Best guess is urine. But thanks to our dead friend, here, for having eaten away the wrappings, Sherlock detected the drugs."

"This is close to where the Jones boy was killed," Slade stated, his tone grim. "Makes me wonder if this stash belonged to him."

"Clay in CSU will give us an accurate time frame for how long this has been buried." Parker inspected the container. "The plastic's pretty eroded. Whatever was in here was very acidic."

"Bag this up."

Parker closed the lid to the box and put it inside a large plastic bag he'd pulled from his waist pack.

"I hope this isn't what the code leads to," Slade said. "There has to be more than one brick of cocaine at stake." Picking up the trowel, Slade started to dig. "Let's see if there is anything else here."

Parker's cell phone chirped. A quick glance at the caller ID sent his heart rate into triple time. He hit the answer button. "Melody?"

"Help."

The barely audible whisper came through the line and grabbed him by the throat, cutting off his air supply.

She was in trouble. Everything inside of him twisted with terror. He couldn't let her down.

"I'm coming!" he ground out.

Melody closed her hand over the phone with equal parts relief and terror. Parker was on his way. He would defeat this monster. But would he arrive in time?

She wasn't sure how much longer she would be able to avoid capture. She was trapped under the bed, her legs tucked up as much as the shallow space would allow. She'd managed to kick her attacker hard enough to make him release her ankle.

Each time he stretched his arm under the bed, trying to grab her, she scooted out of reach. As long as she stayed in the center and remained aware of where he was so she could move, she'd be able to keep from harm until Parker arrived.

Her attacker's growl of frustration echoed through her. The primal rage in that deep roar sent a shiver of dread racing down her spine.

For whatever reason, this man wanted her dead. If he caught her…the future flashed in her mind. A future with Parker, something she'd never imagined before, something she couldn't imagine living without now.

Lord, I beg You, please…

She heard his footsteps retreating to the living room.

She scooted to the head of the bed, her knees and elbows scraping on the rug. Her gun was on the dresser. That was her only hope if Parker didn't show up soon. She inched to the edge of the bed frame.

The sound of something dragging on the carpet sent a fresh wave of fear through her. What was he doing?

"Come out or I'll kill this officer," the harsh voice jolted through the room.

Oh, no. Officer Truman. Melody couldn't let anything happen to her. Without hesitation, she scrambled out from beneath the bed. The intruder held a gun to Officer Truman's head.

"Let her go," Melody demanded.

"Not until you give me it!"

She spread her hands out. "What do you want?"

"Your nephew's watch. Where is it?"

So not what she was expecting. Not that she'd ever been in a situation like this. Not even during training at the police academy. But she knew she needed to remain in control. Unemotional. She took a calming breath. "Daniel's watch? It's a cheap knockoff. Worthless. I don't understand why anyone would want that."

"You don't have to understand. Where is it?"

She needed to buy time for Parker to arrive. "In my purse. Under the bed."

"Get it!"

Dropping back down she wiggled under the bedframe and stretched her arm for her bag. *Slow down,* her mind screamed.

Though her fingers closed around the strap of her purse, she made a show of trying to reach farther.

"Hurry up!"

"I'm trying."

A thump echoed in the room. Thundering steps shook the floor. He yanked her out from under the bed. Officer Truman lay in an unconscious heap near the door.

Jumping to her feet, Melody faced the masked man. A plan formed. It was now or never.

She threw the bag at his face.

He ducked.

She scrambled over the bed, trying to get around him. She needed to get out of the suite. Get help for Truman.

His big hand closed over her arm, jerking her backward.

She tumbled off the bed and landed on her back with a thud on the floor, her head snapping with the impact. Bells rang in her ears. Stars exploded behind her eyes. For a split second, the world dimmed.

She fought to stay conscious. She forced herself upright.

The masked gunman blocked her way to the door. He ripped open her purse and dumped the contents on the bed. He snatched the watch and quickly dissembled the timepiece, pulling the back off. A small, folded piece of paper fell out. He gently undid the folds and held the paper up so the overhead light could shine across it.

Melody squinted to see what was written on

the tiny scrap of paper. She could make out a set of numbers. She had no idea what they meant.

"Finally, the code," the masked gunman exclaimed.

Surprise washed through her. This man must be The Boss. And she'd unknowingly had the code all along. Her nephew must have been the one to steal it. But why? What had he planned to do with the code? Why hide it in his watch? What did it lead to?

The Boss pocketed the paper and raised his weapon, aiming at her head. "Thank you. You've served your purpose."

Melody's heart pitched. Parker. She didn't want to die and leave him. She loved him. But now it was too late. She flinched, bracing herself for the deadly shot that would take her life.

Lord, spare me.

An eruption of barking splintered the air. Sherlock raced into the room, positioning himself between her and the gunman.

Parker blasted through the doorway, his weapon drawn. "Drop your weapon."

Melody's heart leaped.

The Boss spun around. His weapon discharged. The loud bang rocked the room. Parker jerked backward, a red stain spreading from his shoulder and across his chest. He crumpled to the ground.

Horror filled Melody. The bullet missed his vest. Sherlock barked and snarled.

The gunman vaulted over Parker and raced out of the suite. Sherlock chased after him.

Choked with fear, Melody crawled to Parker's side.

He lay still. His eyes closed.

Tears ran down her face. Anguish seared her heart.

"Halt!" Melody heard Slade's voice. Another shot rang out. She could only pray the K-9 captain had stopped the crime lord.

Hands shaking, she gingerly lifted Parker's head to her lap. She smoothed his hair back from his dear face. "Please don't die," she whispered. "I need you."

Sherlock raced back into the room. He nudged his way under her arm and licked Parker's face.

"I love you, Parker." The words broke on a sob. She buried her face against Sherlock's velvety coat.

Within minutes, law enforcement and paramedics filled the hotel suite. Officer Truman was taken out on a gurney. Slade drew her away from Parker to allow the paramedics to tend to him.

"Did you get him?" she asked.

Grim faced, Slade shook his head. "No. He got away. But I'll take him down if it's the last thing I do."

"He—" she broke off when the paramedics lifted Parker onto a gurney. She stepped forward to follow but Slade captured her elbow.

"Melody, I need you here," Slade insisted. "You have to tell me everything that happened."

She knew it was standard procedure for her to give a statement now while the events were fresh in her memory, but her heart didn't want to follow protocol. "Please, let me go with him. This can wait."

For a strained moment she thought he'd refuse. Then he nodded. "Go. I'll take care of Sherlock then come to the hospital and talk to you there."

She hurried to catch up to the paramedics. She held Parker's hand the whole way to the hospital. When they arrived at the E.R. entrance, she was brushed aside by doctors and nurses intent on saving his life. She was too anxious, too upset to sit. She paced the waiting room, praying the whole time beneath her breath.

"Please, Lord, let him live. I'm trusting You to let him live."

"Melody!" Kaitlin rushed to her side and enveloped her in a hug.

More tears pooled in Melody's eyes. She clung to her friend. Soon Melody became aware that others joined them. The whole K-9 unit showed up.

"We're here for you and Parker," Val whispered into her ear as she pulled her into a hug.

Melody managed to croak out a "thank you." These people loved Parker, too. They were a family in a way that she'd never experienced. But today she was one of them.

She belonged. Because of Parker.

A fresh wave of love washed through her. Unknowingly, he'd fulfilled her heart's desire.

Slade arrived and pulled Melody to the side. She told him everything she remembered about the attack and The Boss.

"The code was in Daniel's watch all this time?"

"Yes, sir." She grimaced. "I had no idea."

"None of us did."

"I caught a glimpse of the numbers and letters on the paper," Melody told him. She quickly recited them while Slade wrote them down on a notepad.

"I'll give this to the forensics team and see if they can decode it."

"Sir, I'm sure this has something to do with the Lost Woods."

He nodded. "You're right. Everything keeps coming back to the Lost Woods."

Finally, a doctor in green scrubs entered the waiting room. "You all are here about Detective Adams?"

"Yes," came a resounding chorus of male and female voices.

The doctor broke out in a smile. "I'm happy to say your friend will be fine. The bullet went through his shoulder and didn't hit any vital organs. He'll recover nicely."

Melody sagged with relief. "When can I—we—see him?"

"He's awake now, but a bit groggy. You can go in one at a time. But limit your visit to a minute or two."

"Melody, you go first," Slade said.

Grateful to the captain, she hurried to Parker's room with every intention of telling him she loved him and wanted nothing more in life than to be with him.

She only hoped he'd give her a second chance.

Parker blinked. He was sure the medication was making him hallucinate. He blinked again.

Nope. Melody stood beside his bed, looking disheveled yet remarkably pretty. Tears streaked down her pale cheeks. Her big blue eyes held so much emotion in their swirling depths, he found himself happily growing dizzy staring into her gaze.

"You're safe," he said as his chest expanded with love for her. When he'd walked in and saw that monster aiming at her, it had taken all his self-control not to drop the masked gunman on the spot. His hesitation cost him, but it had saved Melody. No regrets. The price had been well worth paying.

She clutched his hand, her fingers entwining with his. "I'm safe. Thanks to you." She gave him a watery smile. "And Sherlock."

His face darkened with concern. When he tried to sit up, pain shot through him. "Where is he?" he asked between gritted teeth.

She laid a gentle hand on his chest. "Slade took him to the training yard."

Relieved, he sagged back against the pillows. "That's good."

Her gaze caressed him. "I was so scared we'd lose you."

"Not half as much as I was," he countered and suppressed a shudder at the horror of thinking the worst had happened to her. The thought of losing her... "I was afraid I wouldn't make it in time."

"You did." She lifted his hand to her cheek. "I owe you so much."

He winced. He didn't want her here out of gratitude. He wanted her love. "You don't owe me anything."

"I owe you an apology."

"Why?" he asked gruffly.

"Because I was a coward."

"Not true," he said. "You were brave and found a way to call for help. That's not the actions of a coward."

"I trusted God to save me. He sent you."

It made his heart glad to know she'd clung to her faith. "God will never let you down."

"Neither will you. I trust you, Parker. You'll never let me down."

He looked away. "You can't be sure."

She brushed her hand over his forehead. "I'm sure."

Her touch seared him, made him ache in a peculiar way. He met her eyes. "I'm very flawed."

She arched an eyebrow. "What flaws?"

Her trust meant the world to him. But he wanted her love. "But you don't love me."

Dropping her gaze, she tugged at her bottom lip with her teeth. "That's why I owe you the apology."

"I don't understand?"

Lifting her eyes to his, she said, "I wasn't honest with you about how I felt."

"Oh?"

Her expression turned sheepish. "I was too afraid to admit that I love you, too."

Hope ballooned in his chest. "You do?"

She nodded. "I do. And I can't imagine my life without you. I don't want to imagine it."

Her words sent his heart spinning. Fierce emotion pushed any physical pain he felt aside until he was filled with a deep abiding happiness. "I can't imagine my life without *you*. You've become my whole world."

Delight lit up her face. "Me and Sherlock, you mean."

He laughed. "You and Sherlock and maybe one day a couple of kids?"

Her eyes widened, then a soft joyous smile spread across her face. "That sounds like the perfect plan."

He tugged her closer until her lips hovered over his. "Kiss me then and show me you mean it."

"Gladly."

Their lips met. And Parker felt like he was flying on the wings of her love guided by God's hand. And he never wanted to land.

* * * * *

Dear Reader,

Writing a story featuring a dog was new to me. But I fell in love with the beagle Sherlock. He and his handler, Parker Adams made an excellent team. Pairing them up with cold-case detective Melody Zachary was a good fit. Both Parker and Melody had trust issues stemming from their pasts. Using what they learned from each other and drawing on their faith helped them overcome their hurts.

As part of the Texas K-9 Unit, Parker and Sherlock were hot on the trail of the crime syndicate and the mysterious Boss, who had Melody in his sights. Thankfully, they uncovered a part of the mystery revolving around Melody's nephew's death. But the crime lord is still at large. To discover the identity of the villain, read next month's conclusion to the Texas K-9 series in *Lone Star Protector* written by Lenora Worth.

Until we meet again, may God bless you.

Questions for Discussion

1. What made you pick up this book to read? In what ways did it live up to your expectations?

2. What was your first impression of Parker Adams? How would you describe his character?

3. What did you think of Sherlock? Do you own a dog? If so, can you put into words what your pet means to you? If you don't own a pet, why not?

4. What was your first impression of Melody Zachary? How would you describe her? Would she be someone you would want to be friends with? Why?

5. If you read the preceding books in the Texas K-9 series, in what ways did this book surprise you?

6. As Parker and Melody worked together, how did the romance build?

7. Melody had trust issues. Where did those issues stem from? Have you ever had some-

one break your trust? How did you overcome your hurt?

8. Parker was afraid of letting people down. What was at the core of his fear? Is trusting others to love us despite our flaws hard? Why or why not?

9. The scripture in the middle of the book taught Melody her faith had to be active. What does that mean? How can we demonstrate an active faith?

10. What about the setting was clear and appealing? What did you like most about the setting?

11. When did Melody start to realize she had feelings for Parker? Why did she fight her feelings?

12. Parker wanted to maintain a professional distance. Was he able to do so? Why not? When did his feelings change?

13. Melody wanted to belong. In what ways did Parker make her feel like she belonged? In what ways do you belong in your world?

14. Did you notice the scripture in the beginning of the book? What do you think God means

by these words? What application does the scripture have to your life?

15. How did the author's use of language/writing style make this an enjoyable read?

LARGER-PRINT BOOKS!

GET 2 FREE LARGER-PRINT NOVELS PLUS 2 FREE MYSTERY GIFTS

Love Inspired
SUSPENSE
RIVETING INSPIRATIONAL ROMANCE

Larger-print novels are now available...

YES! Please send me 2 FREE LARGER-PRINT Love Inspired® Suspense novels and my 2 FREE mystery gifts (gifts are worth about $10). After receiving them, if I don't wish to receive any more books, I can return the shipping statement marked "cancel." If I don't cancel, I will receive 4 brand-new novels every month and be billed just $5.24 per book in the U.S. or $5.74 per book in Canada. That's a savings of at least 23% off the cover price. It's quite a bargain! Shipping and handling is just 50¢ per book in the U.S. and 75¢ per book in Canada.* I understand that accepting the 2 free books and gifts places me under no obligation to buy anything. I can always return a shipment and cancel at any time. Even if I never buy another book, the two free books and gifts are mine to keep forever.

110/310 IDN F5CC

Name _____ (PLEASE PRINT)

Address _____ Apt. #

City _____ State/Prov. _____ Zip/Postal Code

Signature (if under 18, a parent or guardian must sign)

Mail to the Harlequin® Reader Service:
IN U.S.A.: P.O. Box 1867, Buffalo, NY 14240-1867
IN CANADA: P.O. Box 609, Fort Erie, Ontario L2A 5X3

Are you a current subscriber to Love Inspired Suspense books and want to receive the larger-print edition? Call 1-800-873-8635 or visit www.ReaderService.com.

* Terms and prices subject to change without notice. Prices do not include applicable taxes. Sales tax applicable in N.Y. Canadian residents will be charged applicable taxes. Offer not valid in Quebec. This offer is limited to one order per household. Not valid for current subscribers to Love Inspired Suspense larger-print books. All orders subject to credit approval. Credit or debit balances in a customer's account(s) may be offset by any other outstanding balance owed by or to the customer. Please allow 4 to 6 weeks for delivery. Offer available while quantities last.

Your Privacy—The Harlequin® Reader Service is committed to protecting your privacy. Our Privacy Policy is available online at www.ReaderService.com or upon request from the Harlequin Reader Service.

We make a portion of our mailing list available to reputable third parties that offer products we believe may interest you. If you prefer that we not exchange your name with third parties, or if you wish to clarify or modify your communication preferences, please visit us at www.ReaderService.com/consumerchoice or write to us at Harlequin Reader Service Preference Service, P.O. Box 9062, Buffalo, NY 14269. Include your complete name and address.

LISLPDIR13R

ReaderService.com

Manage your account online!

- Review your order history
- Manage your payments
- Update your address

> *We've designed*
> *the Harlequin® Reader Service*
> *website just for you.*

Enjoy all the features!

- Reader excerpts from any series
- Respond to mailings and special monthly offers
- Discover new series available to you
- Browse the Bonus Bucks catalog
- Share your feedback

Visit us at:

ReaderService.com